Pickles-N-Fries and Fireflies

Rachel Anne Jones

ISBN: 979-8-88653-185-5

Published by Satin Romance
An Imprint of Melange Books, LLC
White Bear Lake, MN 55110
www.satinromance.com

Published in the United States of America.

Cover Design by Caroline Andrus

"The truth is I gave my heart away a long time ago, my whole heart, and I never really got it back."

- *SWEET HOME ALABAMA*

Thank you to Vanessa and Connie for weighing in on the color scheme. You've got great taste!

I dedicate this story first and foremost to Douglas, and secondly to Isaac, Amy, Isabel, and Abby. A special thank you to Isaac and Sandy, for your vital input to the title of the book! I am also thankful to all the inspiring meet-cutes who were so generous to share your stories with me; thank you so much. (You know who you are.)

To all those who grew up in a small town and truly understand the phrase "too close for comfort", and to the joys of living in a close-knit community where everyone is your neighbor.

Lastly, I dedicate this story to future generations; love is patient and love is kind. It's as simple as making time for others and taking time to smell the roses.

As always, thank you, Nancy, for taking a chance on me as an author, and thank you Ashley and Caroline for your killer book covers!

Prelude To Love

(AND HALF-VALENTINE'S DAY)

"What is love?
Lady don't hurt me
Don't hurt me no
More.." nah, just kiddin'

Sit back and hold tight
To the reins – love's
Comin' at ya like
Blood in your veins

I've got stories that'll
Make you weep,
Laugh, cry, and sing
They all end with one little ring

Funny how a tiny band of gold
Holds secrets, sorrows,
Laughter, and years
Of marital bliss, and more than a few tears

Herein lies the mystery
That will captivate the reader
Meet-cute stories of your neighbors,

PRELUDE TO LOVE

Ordinary people like you and me

What makes life extraordinary
Has us laughing, weeping,
Singing. Take Notice. Pay
Heed. Love is celebration, desperation, sacrifice.

If only Love was like a paint
By number; follow
The steps and you get
A vibrant prize in the end

But they say anything
Worth havin' takes hard work
And dedication. If it's too easy,
Is it worth savin'?

Here's your challenge
I'm throwin' it down
match each mystery Couple
to their unique beginning
Guess 'em all right and collect your winnings!
-Maddie Dill
The Weekly Chase

"You can take the girl out of the honky-tonk, but you can't take the honky-tonk out of the girl."

- *SWEET HOME ALABAMA*

One

Mason French leans forward on the bar stool as he hovers over the newspaper, scanning the poem with a bemused expression on his face. "Maddie Dill," he mutters under his breath. "Wouldn't that be somethin' if she came back here, a place she swore she'd never set foot in again?"

Ron and Casey's conversation about the latest weather report per the Farmer's Almanac for the next winter comes to a screeching halt. "Did you just say Maddie Dill?" Tall, blond Ron announces in a voice loud enough for Mason to shrink just a hair.

"Shut it down, Ron," Mason mumbles to his friend as he glances around the room, feeling all exposed. "Geez. You're so loud."

Green-eyed Casey crosses his arms in his signature flannel before leaning back to smirk at the two of them. "Shoot, Mason. You must not get out at all these days. Haven't you heard?"

Mason's stomach tightens with anticipation at the thought of any news about Maddie Dill, the one who got away. "Heard what?"

Casey gives him a sly grin. "Word has it she's comin' back for the summer."

Ron nods with too much enthusiasm, as far as Mason's

concerned. "Yep. Her mom's MS has gotten bad again and so Maddie's comin' home. She's even doin' an internship down at the newspaper, though I heard her and Shelly don't see eye-to-eye on much."

"I don't believe it." Mason shakes his head and taps his finger on the newspaper. "Well, I mean I believe Maddie's plenty opinionated. There's no question about that. But she swore she'd never be back once she graduated high school, and it's not like Maddie to go back on her word." Mason swallows hard when he recalls the last thing she yelled at him when they were both sixteen. "I'm never talking to you again, Mason French!" He stares off into the distance. She was way too good at making good on her promise. Nothing stings worse than your best friend literally giving you the silent treatment for the rest of your high-school days. He shakes his head to clear his memory.

Ron stares Mason down. "What went down with you two, anyway? You were glued together at the hip and then it was like you were complete strangers."

"Yeah. What happened?" Casey grins. "Did you two get it on? That'll ruin a friendship real quick."

Mason's fists clench. He glares at Casey. "That's not what happened. You're not even close."

Ron leans in. "Then what was it that split you two apart?"

Mason flips the newspaper over. He can't read Maddie's words of poetry on the page a second longer, but she's got one thing right. Love is pain, especially when you're stupid enough to fall for Maddie Dill.

Mason takes a deep breath. It's definitely time to change the subject. He glances around the spacious bar room. He's surprised to see so many of the people he grew up with in it who will soon be potential customers. He'll be doing business with them before too long now that he's agreed to take over his grandfather's business, which is the last thing he thought he would do. He stares down at his hands in disbelief once more. He's filled with annoyance all over again. It sucks being the only one of his siblings who has any sense of fulfilling family obligations. He raises his head to find Ron and Casey staring at him with expectation in their eyes. Mason forces a grin in their direction. "You guys remember all the times we tried to sneak in here for a drink?" He shakes his head again. "Like everyone didn't know we were underage. This town is so small."

Ron does a table tap. "Yep. It's small all right, too small for secrets." He grins at Mason like he knows something he shouldn't. "Except for maybe your secret."

Mason fidgets. "What're you talkin' about? I don't have any secrets."

"You tellin' me you haven't been harborin' a crush on Maddie Dill all these years?" Ron winks at Mason, who wants to punch him in the face. "I hear she's single."

Mason's anger dissipates as his ears perk up. "Wasn't she, uh, wasn't she engaged to some big-shot real estate guy or something like that?"

Ron's face lights up, and Mason does an inward groan. He recognizes that look. Ron's about to spill tea. "She was engaged like less than a month ago, but she found out he cheated on her, and she gave him the boot."

"It was bad." Casey looks down at the table. "The guy was a real tool. I can't believe he'd do somethin' like that less than a month before they were to be married. He left her with a helluva mess. She had to cancel all the plans and get all the refunds, including their honeymoon cruise."

Mason's confused. "How come I didn't hear about any of this?"

Ron looks all sheepish. "Maddie kind of put the word out that she didn't want the news reaching certain people." He tugs at his collar.

Mason scratches his head. "That must be why I didn't get an official wedding invitation either."

"You didn't get an invite to Maddie's weddin'?" Ron's blue eyes widen in surprise. "She invited our whole class practically."

Mason takes a long swallow of beer, feeling more than a little wounded. "Well, that's a pretty sucky deal. That's too bad for Maddie."

"Yeah, I 'spose." Casey grins. "It must not have been too hard on her, though. I heard she's lookin' pret-ty fine." Casey smiles at Mason, looking all ornery. "Maddie must have some pret-ty strong feelin's for you, if she couldn't even invite you to the weddin'."

Mason stares at the floor. "Yeah, somethin' like that." He mumbles his response. Everything's quiet for about half a second.

Ron slugs Casey in the arm. "Hey. You remember the night of the bonfire and Maddie showed up in that bikini, shakin' us all up?"

Casey coughs a little. "Yep. Up until then we all thought she was a tomboy. Nobody knew she was hidin' her goodies under her hoodies." He chuckles at his own joke.

"That was so lame." Ron takes a sip of beer and sets it down while rolling his eyes.

"I thought it was funny," Casey replies.

Ron's whole face changes like he just solved a mystery. "Wasn't that the night she stopped talking to you, Mason?"

Mason takes another long drink of his Miller Lite and tugs at his collar as he sets it down on the table. "You know what guys? There's no need to rehash the past. High school was a long time ago. You're makin' me feel old."

"So you're tellin' me that if Maddie Dill walked in here tonight, you'd have nothin' to say to her 'cause it's all in the past? Forgotten." He raises his eyebrows in challenge.

Mason throws out his arms. "It doesn't matter 'cause that's never gonna happen. Maddie Dill wouldn't set foot in here. This bar is the social center of our Podunk little town, the one place she swore off."

Casey laughs out loud and points behind Mason's shoulder. "You're right about one thing. Your friendship was a long time ago. You don't know Maddie near as well as you think."

Mason's curiosity gets the better of him. He ducks his head to the side to look at the front door of the bar that flies open, banging the side wall. His breath hitches as the only girl who could literally bring him to his knees, Maddie Dill, strides through the front door of the Red Dog Saloon. If Mason didn't know better, he'd swear a calf just kicked him in the stomach. His gaze is caught. He can't catch his breath. The mood lighting may be dim, but there's no mistaking those big brown eyes and that fly-away red hair that lifts just right as the screen door slams shut behind her.

"Dude. Stop starin'." Ron punches his arm.

Mason's head is cranked. "I can't." No sooner do those words leave Mason's mouth than Maddie's eyes meet his. Her brown eyes widen just enough to show appreciation that quickly turns to scorn and annoyance. She flicks her head to the side. Mason whips around to face Casey sitting at his right, but he's really watching Maddie slide into a booth. Mason frowns as he sees Zach sidle up to Maddie's table in all of ten seconds. "Since when did the bartender leave the bar to take a drink order?" Mason growls.

Ron snorts. "It's Maddie Dill and she's on the rebound. Need I say more?"

Mason scowls. "Doesn't Zach have a wife and kids at home?"

"Yep," Casey said, grinning, "but they ain't here."

Ron nudges Mason's elbow. "Hey, you want us to walk you over there an' say 'hi'."

Mason rolls his eyes. "What are we, a bunch of women? If I want to say hello, I will." He glances at Maddie who still hasn't looked in his direction. Maddie fills the corner of his eye as she sits on the edge of her booth in the somewhat crowded bar. Part of him jangles with anticipation, but the other part wants to turn tail and hide. Mason feels so unprepared. He had no idea she was in town, and he was not ready to see her when all he can remember is that night at the bonfire. It was their sophomore year.

His heart was in his chest. He was finally going to tell Maddie he wanted to be more than friends, but he couldn't find the words, so he followed his instincts. He leaned in to kiss her. She jumped up and took off, but not before he caught the look of horror and panic in her eyes. That was the day he lost his best friend and the only girl he'd ever loved.

Ron shakes his head. "Just go say 'hi'. It's no big deal. You've known Maddie since you were kids. Remember when you used to call her Dill Pickle and she called you French Fry on account of your last name is French and one time you grabbed an electric fence and gave yourself quite the shock?"

Casey laughs out loud. "Your grandpa laughed so hard he almost fell over when he told me that story. And he'd really get to goin' when he got to the part when he managed to get out his tellin' you, 'you've been French-fried'."

Mason nods his head. "Thanks for that reminder, guys. Trust me, I did not find this event near as humorous as he did, and when I made the mistake of relaying the story to Maddie at school because I was trying to impress her with my death-defying story, she found it as funny as my grandpa did and dubbed me 'French Fry' and the name stuck." Mason rolls his eyes. "So naturally, I had to tease her back and so I called her Dill Pickle. And you all know how well Maddie takes teasing. I was like, 'if you're going to make fun of me, I'll make fun of you.'"

Casey takes a swig of beer and shakes his head. "That's how you guys became Pickles-n-Fries? All I know is as long as I can remember no one got one of you without the other. Ever. You two were inseparable, which is good, because you had a big mouth and not everyone thought you were funny." He grins again. "It's a good thing Maddie was there. She saved you from more than one ass-beatin'."

"Yeah, probably," he reluctantly agrees, his face hot at the memories of Maddie and her swinging fists on the playground.

Ron stares past Casey at Maddie sitting in the booth with Andrea, another girl from their high school years. He's all smiles as he looks over at Mason. "I always thought the two of you would end up together."

Mason's stomach tightens. "Why do you say that?"

Ron shrugs. "I don't know. Best friends usually do." Ron

stares Mason down. "Are you tellin' me the two of you never hooked up, like not even in college?"

"Dude, we just had this conversation." Mason coughs. "You guys know Maddie's not like that. We're just friends. I..I would never."

Casey laughs and claps Mason on the shoulder. "Re-lax, French Fry. Ron didn't mean anythin' by it." He squeezes Mason's arm. "Besides, we all know she shot you down in high school. That had to sting."

Mason's jaw tightens. He feels played and he doesn't like it. "What? How did you know?"

Casey shoots Ron a look. Ron grins. Mason frowns even more. He starts to stand up. "Whatever. The two of you always did like gossip a little too much and that's all this is."

Ron knocks on the table. "You don't believe us? Fine." He leans in again. "One night Maddie got drunk down here at the bar after some weddin' she went to alone. Apparently, she started talkin' about the time you tried to kiss her and how she kind of wished she would have because after that you acted all weird. She went on about how much she missed your friendship, and you were the best friend she ever had." Ron shakes his head. "We were all shocked. It wasn't like Maddie to tell her business, and we honestly didn't think she had it in her to get all sentimental."

Mason wants to walk away, but he can't stop listening. He plops back down. He can't believe Maddie wanted him to kiss her or that she announced it down at the bar. She had to know it would get back to him, right? Mason knocks his fist on the table. "I didn't stop talkin' to her. She stopped talkin' to me."

Mason casts another glance in her direction. He takes in her long red hair, trailing her narrow back while she sits in the booth waving her arms wildly about. Mason grins as his grandpa's favorite words to describe Maddie, "bleeding heart liberal" run through his mind. Mason breathes out slowly. Maddie's just as gorgeous as she's always been, and if her waving hands are any indication, those gorgeous lips of hers are going a mile a minute. That hasn't changed much either.

"Hey," Ron says.

Mason snaps out of his gazing at Maddie. "What?"

Ron looks all ornery and scheming. Mason wants to walk away. "A whole summer's long enough to get to know her better don't you think?"

"I guess." Mason shrugs. "But I'll be busy and so will she. What are you gettin' at?"

Ron chugs his beer and sets it down. "I bet you a hundred bucks you can't hook up with Maddie while she's here."

Mason's out of his chair. His finger is in Ron's face. "Say one more word like that about Maddie, Ron and I'll wipe this floor with you," he threatens.

Casey's hand falls on Mason's arm. "Cool down. It was a joke." Casey stares hard at Ron. "Right? It was a joke."

Ron shrugs it off, but his face is full of annoyance. "Sure, man. Whatever."

"Ron took it too far, alright," Casey says, "but what about a kiss? That's pretty harmless." Mason swallows hard. *Sure, it's as harmless as the only thing I've dreamed about for half my life.* Casey clears his throat. "I bet you forty bucks you can't get a kiss from her before she leaves the bar tonight."

"You're on." Mason grins ear to ear and turns to walk away.

"She has to kiss you. That's what I meant," Casey calls out.

Mason spins back around to face Casey. "It's too late. You can't change your words now." He gives them a wink. "I'm goin' in."

Casey turns back to Ron. "Looks like Maddie will be wipin' the floor with Mason tonight."

Ron pouts in his chair. "I can't believe he was gonna kick my ass over a girl."

Casey's green eyes light up with delight. "You better hope Mason doesn't tell Maddie what you said about her, or she'll be comin' for ya too."

Two

Mason hesitates as he slinks into the booth right behind Maddie. He leans back. He's feeling all kinds of stupid. He knows his male pride has never let him down before, just like he knows if a bet is what it takes for him to take a bite out of a sour Dill Pickle, he'll do it. He just has to get up his nerve. Mason glances over at Ron. He catches his friend's "you'll never do it" smirk on his face right before Ron shakes his head as if to say, "Never in a million years."

Mason scooches to the outside edge of the booth. He feels like nothing less than a creeper as he smells the light scent of flowers. His knees buckle just a little even though he's sitting. Maddie hasn't changed so much. She still wears the same perfume that drives him crazy, the one that takes him right back to Maddie's fifteenth birthday and the dance they shared before everyone else showed up to the party. They were in her room dancing to "Don't Stop Believing" by Journey. It was Maddie's favorite song.

He glances down at the floor. Her flowered Lariats catch his eye. He laughs to himself. She wore those things everywhere. Mason used to tease her about sleeping in them. Something hits the floor. It rolls along the wood and stops when it hits his shoe. All of a sudden, Maddie is everywhere.

She's so focused on chasing the ring that she doesn't see

Mason as she leans over in his space to grab for the ring. Her other hand grabs his knee for balance as she kind of falls over him to keep from face planting into the floor.

Her red hair covers the calf of his blue jeans. Her glazed eyes focus a little as she stares up at him. Her grip on his knee tightens while her other hand closes around the ring on the floor. Mason can't stop staring at Maddie Dill, his childhood friend, his co-conspirator, his first crush, and then his enemy. She's back and she's a knock-out. Mason doesn't know what to feel or think. The only conscious thought he has is that he's speechless.

As Maddie sees him see her, time slows down, but it speeds up at the same time. Her eyes roam over the front of him and they widen just enough to let Mason know she's interested. Mason braces himself. It's been a long time since he grabbed hold of an electric fence, much less tried to one.

———

Maddie swallows hard as she stares up at Mason. What does he think he's doing waltzing back into her life like he never left and why does he have to look so good doing it?

Scattered thoughts fill her muddled brain. She can't believe she was just sitting at a table at the Red Dog Saloon, a new bar in her old hometown, the one place she swore she'd never set foot in again. And then to add insult to injury French Fry shows up lookin' as handsome as sin. Maddie bites her lip. She also can't believe that thought just rolled itself across her $40,000.00 educated brain. No thanks to the dang ole' Republicans who probably went to college for free back in the day but now think it's a good idea to charge everyone bookoo bucks just because they can. This was a conversation she was just trying to have with an old classmate, Andrea, who appeared more than a little bored, but Maddie just kept going in her usual ranting-Maddie style.

"Maddie Dill." Mason's voice is a little deeper than the last time they spoke. Holy smokes. His baritone burns her ears and other parts of her that she'd just as soon shut down. "I'd give anything to know what you're thinkin' right now."

Maddie prays her cheeks don't flush with shame. She's thinking a few things, but there's only one she'll admit to. She takes a breath or two as she wills herself to keep looking at Mason, who turns her inside out.

"I...was just tellin' Andrea over here that a college degree used to be a necessity if you wanted to get ahead in the world. Now it's a necessary evil if you want to tread water in the drowning pool of getting by which means you work until you're eighty-five just to pay off your student loans."

Mason blinks a few times. By the look on his face, Maddie guesses that's the last thing he thought she would say. She fights her grin of triumph that pops out, anyway.

"Is that right?" Mason clears his throat and lays a hand over Maddie's that's still attached to his knee.

She jerks her hand back, grabs hold of the booth and pulls herself up from her semi-squat. "That's right."

He peeks around the corner at Andrea who sits across from Maddie. He bumps Maddie's hip with his right shoulder in the process. He looks up at Maddie. "I'd say Andrea's a little past the point of hearing you."

"Yeah, I suppose so. She's been makin' drunk eyes at the tired cowboy in the corner who might be five years away from a nursing home, but who am I to judge?" Maddie rolls her eyes. "I *knew* she was hitting on Mr. Brown back in high school. I guess she's always liked 'em old."

Mason coughs. "Maddie, how much have you had to drink?"

Maddie's hand flies to her mouth. "Did I just say all that out loud?"

Mason nods his head. "Yep."

Andrea scoots out of the booth on shaky feet as she stares Maddie down. By the look on Andrea's face, she's not as drunk as Maddie thought. "Well, shoot and damn it. I always was a little too good at being awkward," Maddie mutters into the air as Andrea stomps away.

Mason stands up next to Maddie before almost sitting on her before bumping her again, managing to awkwardly nudge her further into the booth. He follows her flowery scent as he scoots in beside her.

Maddie peeks around Mason at Andrea, who now sits in a booth with Teri, another old classmate. Maddie flinches as she sees Andrea and her eyes-of-flint staring over at her though Maddie can't really blame her. Maddie ducks behind Mason once more.

"Well, Andrea and I were classmates, but we were never the best of friends. I think the reunion we just had can wait another five to ten years before it repeats itself."

Mason chuckles. "I suppose it will. You always were way too good at holding a grudge." Maddie flinches at his words that hit her right between the eyes. She knows exactly what he's talking about, and she can't believe even now that she gave him the silent treatment as long as she did just like she can't believe Mason's manly hand resting on the table that's way too close to her front.

Maddie feels a bit defensive. "I was just a girl. It was a long time ago. It seems rather silly now, don't you think? I mean, you have a chance to be the bigger person, not that you aren't the bigger person, because you totally are in every sense of the word. Not that I'm saying you're too big, you're just right but you know what I'm sayin'." Her voice trails off as Mason closes in on her.

His shoulder bumps hers as his breath falls on her ear. Maddie's pretty sure none of this would affect her so severely had she not already downed a few shots and a couple of whiskey sours in the span of ten minutes. As it is, she's feeling pretty warm, and she thinks that happened before her best friend turned nemesis turned hottie invaded her space, but she's not sure. "Does that mouth of yours ever quit, Dill Pickle?"

He's all suggestive and lean-y. His breath reeks of rum. She practically falls sideways into the wall to get away from him before she goes up in flames.

He doesn't get the hint. He keeps inching toward Maddie until his thigh lines up with hers under the table. He lays one hand on bench beside her leg while his other hand practically grips the side of the table. "How ya doing, Mad-die Dill?" His foot nudges hers and his fingers reach over to play with her trembling hand. She feels hot as a shot of Fireball.

"What're you doin', French Fry?" she croaks. His steady grey eyes are all happy and teasing. "I'm shaking your hand. Isn't that what old friends do, Mad-die." The word 'friends' sounds as hard as marble coming out of his mouth.

She takes her hand from his. "That's not a handshake, and I'm not your friend."

He looks a little hurt, but then his face changes. He licks his lips. "That's good, Maddie. That's real good, because I don't do this with my friends."

She looks all confused. "What don't you do?"

He snags the rest of drink Andrea left behind. He downs the rum and coke. His hand goes to the back of her neck and his thumb strokes the back of her ear. His other hand frames the side of her face and his lips hover for a split second as his eyes look into hers, as if to ask permission or apologize. She's not sure which. Then his lips are on hers and she can't think of anything else but Mason. The kiss goes on and her head spins. His arms wrap around her like unbreakable steel. His big strong hand is on her neck and the other is on the small of her back. He yanks her flush up against him and wraps his hand around the bottom of her shirt, bunching it up. Maddie goes up in flames.

His lips are magical. His hot breath fills her mouth. He tastes like rum and coke. She can't help but wonder how they fit so well together and how her hands got under his shirt. Catcalls and whistles blister her dulled eardrums. She slowly but surely extricates herself from his marvelous hands. She can barely look him in the eye. It doesn't help that he's got the cat-that-swallowed-the-canary look going on. She can't believe she forgot how his grey eyes measure her from her toes to her nose. She hates that he's staring at her like there's no tomorrow or how much she likes it. A couple of guys walk by. This hardly registers on her radar, currently tuned into one station-Mason French and his delectable lips-but the four twenties on the table do. Mason looks at the money like it's a snake about to strike. She swallows hard. "Am I a bet, Mason?"

He stares at the table, willing it to morph into some black hole and swallow him up. "It's not like that, Maddie. I wanted to." He stops talking.

She knows the answer to her question, but she has to hear him say it. "Was kissing me a bet?"

His confidence runs for the door. He looks like he might cry, and she knows it's no act. He always was the sensitive type. "You have to understand," he begs. "I meant every part of what just happened between us."

"Damn stupid small towns and everybody knowing everybody's business," she growls as she plants her feet on Mason's backside and kicks him out of the booth. She wants to fall through the floor right now. He barely keeps his butt off the floor as he leans back on the palms of his hands in a semi-crab walk. She snatches up two twenties and waves it in his upturned face. "Forty dollars," she hollers. She'll be darned if she's going to lose face in her hometown bar in front of their high school alumni. "Forty dollars is the going rate for a kiss from Maddie Dill," she yells out as she holds her forty dollars high.

She turns to face him once again. By this time, he's managed to stand up. She'll be danged if she lets on how his kiss turned her inside out. Her hand flies out of its own accord and slaps his cheek. Hard. She leaves a handprint on the side of his perfectly chiseled jaw resting beneath a set of grey eyes and dirty blonde hair that's just shaggy enough to whisper lumber jack. She hopes she's not drooling as she fights the urge to reach out a soft hand to cool the heat she just left behind. She stares him down and curses Mason for bein' the only boy who could stir up such emotions in her and for bein' the only boy who made her want to trace his lips with her thumb because they're absolute perfection. His frown grows deeper by the second. His eyes smart. She knows she hurt him in more ways than one, but she can't bring herself to feel bad about it.

Darn French Fry and his stupid betting mouth and darn my quick temper that knows no limits, she thinks to herself right before she steps back and points in his general direction. "French Fry. You won your bet. You got your money. You'll stay away from me if you know what's good for you."

Mason rubs his red cheek and stares back at her. "When have I ever known what's good for me when it comes to you?" he challenges, making her want him even more. Her breath hitches as he takes a step toward her. She wonders how long she can fight the madness between them.

"Mason," she starts. Whatever words were coming next, stop on the tip of her tongue. She can't get past his grey-eyed smolder. She breaks their gaze and clears her throat before looking back at him. She lays a hand on his chest to stop him from getting any closer. "Whatever you think just started didn't. Don't go gettin' any ideas. I'm here for the summer and for my mom. That's it," she vows.

His hot hand covers hers. His jaw tightens. He stares at her through narrowed eyes, but his lips slowly form a smirk that is way sexier than it should be. "I see your dill pickle still has its bite," he teases before giving her a wink. "That's alright. I like it spicy." She bites her lip to keep her jaw from dropping. Mason's learned a few tricks since high school. He's playin' dirty, and she likes it a little too much. He grabs the two twenties she left on the table and waves them above his head. He slaps it in her hand. "It wasn't a bet," he yells before leaning closer to her face. "Not to me. It wasn't a bet to me. I wanted that kiss." His voice is all soft and low.

His words steal her breath. All she wants is to return for seconds. She tears her eyes from his lips. "Stop coming at me French Fry unless you want to get burned. I mean it."

MYSTERY COUPLE

WHO KNEW COLOR GUARD FORMATION COULD BE SO ENCHANTING

We met at band camp. I was 15 and he was 17. We went to separate high schools in a big city, but that day we were competing drum majors. I think I saw him first, the "hot guy in shades" that caught many of my friends' eyes. While the small crowd of girls was attracted to him, I thought he seemed a little too full of himself. To make matters worse we were thrown into a group activity together and I was put in charge! Now I had to prove myself to a bunch of strangers and get them to listen to me. It wasn't going well at all but then the hot guy in the shades stepped in to help me. He quickly won me over with his charm and I was pleasantly surprised to discover he was a pretty nice guy. A friendship soon began between the two of us and it lasted past the end of the week of band camp; even when I returned to my high school, and he returned to his.

A few years later we ended up at the same college and we began seeing each other. Twenty-three years later we are still married, have four wonderful children, and two busy careers. It all started with a passing glance across a field of noisy horns at band camp. Love can be as quiet as a whisper or as loud as a cymbal.

-Maddie Dill
The Daily Chase

Three

Mason's on his way out of the bar when a big hand slaps him on the back. He turns to see Chad Merk, his childhood bully, otherwise known as Merk the Jerk. The nickname stuck, courtesy of Maddie Dill and her ability to shoot from the hip. Mason is puzzled. He doesn't understand why Chad is smiling in his general direction.

"Way to go Mase. I didn't know you had it in ya." Chad smacks Mason on the butt and Mason jumps a little before giving an inward shiver. He can't believe he ever wanted a butt smack from Chad. It's so weird.

Chad yanks out a chair. "Have a seat." Mason sits down slowly. Chad pulls a tab. Mason can hardly believe Chad's friendliness or familiarity with calling him "Mase," but his mind is still stuck on what just happened with Maddie. She always could make him forget where he was or what he was doing. "Here, have a White Claw," Chad mutters as he goes to hand it to Mason, who wills himself not to flinch and lean away like a spaz to avoid being slammed in the face with a cold can from Merk the Jerk. Some habits are hard to break.

Mason reaches slowly for the can before he wraps his hand around it and takes a sip. He can't help but think that tonight is full of surprises. Maddie isn't the only one who's changed since he saw her last. He can hardly believe when comparing the two of them Chad is more welcoming.

Mason takes Chad in, noticing that he looks a little shorter and a lot smaller. "Man, seeing Maddie and the light in her eyes as she got all fired up right before she kicked me out of her booth brought back so many memories. You remember the time we put a tack on our least favorite teacher's chair to see if she could feel anything between her big caboose and those thick corduroy skirts she was so fond of wearing?"

Chad nods his head and chuckles. "Yep, yep. That was classic."

Mason laughs and slowly relaxes. "Or how 'bout the time me and Maddie, with the help of Merk the…" he stops talking and looks Chad in the eye, half expecting to be punched in the shoulder or the face.

Chad just ducks his head. "Hey, dude. I'm sorry for bein' such a jerk back in the day."

Mason takes a long drink before setting it down. "That's alright." They share an awkward moment of silence. "Well, anyway, remember the time we hid the school piano in the upstairs library and convinced everyone we rolled if off the bridge outside of town? That was classic."

Chad nods and laughs right along with him. "Yep. You and I were long-time enemies, thanks to Maddie, but our shenanigans never failed to bring us together at times." Chad gets all serious. "You knew that, right? You were my competition. With Maddie."

"What?" Mason feels like someone clubbed him upside the head.

Chad's face is full of skepticism. "Are you tellin' me you really didn't know why I couldn't stand you?" Chad shakes his head. "For a smart guy, you can be a real idiot." Chad takes a drink of his White Claw and makes a face. "I guess you were so busy chasing her you couldn't see anyone else." Chad pounds a fist on the table and holds up his can. "Here's to chasin' Maddie."

"To chasin' Maddie," Mason said and clinks his can against Chad's. Mason studies Chad with a fair amount of skepticism.

Chad laughs out loud. "You know I'm gettin' married, right?"

Mason feels even more like an idiot, and he didn't think that was possible. "Um, no. I didn't. I'm sorry, man. I mean, congratulations."

Chad nods his head and grins. "Thanks. Your invite should be at your mom's house. We sent them out a while back."

Mason nods again. He feels ridiculous that he can't think of a thing to say. He can't believe Merk the Jerk is getting married or that he's invited to their wedding. "Cool, cool." He stares at the counter in silence until it hits him. "Who are you marrying? Is she from here?"

Chad grins and shakes his head. He finishes off his White Claw and smacks Mason's shoulder. "Dude. I thought you knew. It's Nicole. We've been dating since high school. She never came to the dances because her dad was super strict, and she lived like three hours away." He pauses before eyeing Mason with an ornery look. "You should bring Maddie as your plus one. That'd be somethin'."

"Yeah, maybe." The feeling of a small truck hitting him runs through his mind when Mason thinks of going to a wedding with Maddie.

"Hey, remember the time you two had that old-school Sherlock Holmes local deputy chasing down his own license plate for an entire day after someone downtown reported $50.00 went missing from the local candy store?" Chad leans back in his chair. "That was epic." Chad shakes his head back and forth. "You two really had some guts when it came to playin' pranks."

"Yeah. At the end of the day, the candy store owner figured out he accidentally dropped the fifty bucks which hit the floor and slid beneath the counter where no one could see it. It was only when he was doing his routine floor sweeping that the fifty-dollar bill came unwedged from its hiding place. He called up Officer Flintstone as we liked to call him because he was from the stone ages, to report the missing fifty dollars had been found so there was no need to chase down the license plate of the one car that happened through town with out-of-county plates. But by that time the old dog police officer had figured out he was chasing his own tail, so to speak, and he didn't speak another word about the whole thing." Mason takes another drink. "Those were some good times."

Mason stares at the bar's front door. He can still see Maddie's backside swinging to and fro as she walked away from him. He touches his face, which is half numb from the alcohol, he thinks, but he's not entirely sure. He can't feel her slap anymore but it still stings. He mentally kicks himself. What in the world made him make good on a stupid bet? And why did he think for a second Ron and Casey would keep their bet on the down low and that she wouldn't figure it out?

"Why'd you kiss her?" Chad's voice interrupts Mason's stray thoughts of Maddie.

"Excuse me?"

"Tonight. Was it just a bet?" There was a time Mason wouldn't trust Chad any farther than he could throw him, but Chad seems different now. More honest and grown up. Mason thinks being engaged agrees with Chad, and he needs someone to talk to.

He clears his throat. "I suppose it was the need to clear up unfinished business and the fear that she might get away again that had me chasing her so hard." He taps his fingers on the table. "I've wanted to taste Maddie's lips ever since she denied my attempt the first time. It was her sixteenth birthday and we'd been out swimming all day at the lake. Remember that?"

Chad nods. "Heck, yes. She was wearing that tiny bikini. It drove me nuts. That was the first time I'd seen her look like that."

Mason breathes out and feels a little better that he wasn't the only one who was brought to his knees about her daring transformation. "Tell me about it. I'd been having other feelings for Maddie ever since she went and ruined things between us by developing curves that I couldn't ignore no matter how hard I tried. That excuse for a swimming suit didn't help matters. So we were sitting by the campfire eating our s'mores. Most everyone else had taken off, and it was just me and Maddie."

He stops talking for a minute. Even though it's been almost seven years ago, it's still embarrassing. "You ever think you're reading someone all right, like you're getting a green light, and they're on red? Like big time."

Chad grins. "Yep. A few times."

"Well, that's what happened to me that day. Maddie was sitting there all serious and staring into the fire. I was thinking I finally had her alone and we could talk. She looked over at me and asked me if I'd ever kissed a girl. I thought that meant she was interested, so I scooted closer to her and kind of went in for the kiss. Maddie hopped off that log so fast. She coughed a little bit and told me she wasn't talking about us. She was talking about the new boy, Jeremy."

"Jeremy?" Chad looks all confused. "I don't remember a Jeremy."

Mason swats at Chad's arm. "Yes, you do. He was quiet and he loved music. Anyway, Maddie was just *fascinated* with him." Mason takes another drink. "Even though Jeremy and I had barely spoken two words to each other, and he had no idea Maddie wanted to kiss him, he'd just crossed the line with me. I'd laughed a little after she shot me down and I tried to recover from my moment of humiliation, but after that day, things were different between us. She stopped leaning on me and touching my arm like she used to when we were kidding around. There was tension. It made everything uncomfortable. It felt kind of like a livewire, but it was ten times stronger than being buzzed by that electric fence. I liked it but I didn't. I never knew what would happen next between us and the distance just slowly grew from there. It wasn't long and she stopped talking to me altogether."

"Well, don't give up on her." Chad slaps Mason's shoulder again. "It sounds like she means a lot to you, and you still have unfinished business. That's all I can tell ya."

Mason stands up and sticks out his hand.

Chad stands up, slaps his hand, and gives Mason a huge

bro-hug. Mason tenses up and waits for Chad to crack his ribs about the time Chad lets go. "It was good to see you, man."

"You too, Chad. I'll see you at your wedding." Mason walks out the front door of the bar feeling totally confused. He can't believe he just opened up like that to Chad or that they're kind of friends. But mostly Mason can't believe Chad had a crush on Maddie.

"Maddie Dill," Mason mutters as he stumbles down the middle of the empty street. He's thinking it feels too much like what just happened. Maddie left a bad taste in his mouth and a pain in his chest as well as on his face. He grins. Maddie always could pack a mean wallop. And just like the last time, he wonders when he'll see her again and if she'll forgive him. He can't help but grin at the thought. At least this time, he gave her a reason to be mad.

Four

"Stupid lying Mason and his stupid kissing lips and stupid me for enjoying every bit of it. I can't believe he made me a bet," Maddie mutters into the cool, night air. She can't help but smile a little at the eighty dollars clutched in her hand as she walks her drunk butt down the street to her friend Alex's house. Maddie knows she's too wasted to drive home and that her tiny hometown doesn't have an Uber or Lyft service. The only kind of transportation is the short bus parked outside the Senior Citizen Center, and it doesn't run at midnight. She laughs out loud at the thought of borrowing Amber's bus to drive home. Something tells her the senior center would not forgive her for pulling that sort of prank. She texts her mom.

MADDIE:

Staying at Alex's. C u tomorrow.

She pulls the ring from her pocket and puts it on her finger again. She holds it up beneath the streetlights, admiring its sparkle. "Well, Jeff, I kind of cheated on you tonight but it doesn't count because we're not together anymore." She breathes in deep and holds up her hand again. "You sure have good taste in jewelry, though."

She spins around a few times in the middle of the street

before stopping to look up as if waiting for some kind of answer. "Is it cheating if you don't tell your fiancé about the one guy who meant so much to you if you weren't speaking at the time?" She swallows hard and heads toward Alex's again. "Mason was a part of my life that belonged only to me. There's nothing wrong with that." She slows her walk to a shuffle. "And now he's back, and man can he kiss." She giggles to herself.

Maddie sneaks in Alex's backdoor. She tries to be extra quiet. Alex has a new baby, and Maddie doesn't want to wake either of them. She tiptoes down the stairs to the spare room. She flops down on the bed, kicks off her shoes, and shimmies out of her skintight jeans. Her boy shorts are more comfortable to sleep in. She touches her lips right as she drifts off. She is irritated with her smile that creeps out at the memory of Mason's kiss. He sure knows how to kiss a girl. The longer she lays there the more she gets annoyed. She knows she's not sleeping now, not when her mind is stuck on Mason French. She whips out her phone. She wonders who he's been seeing.

She finds him on Facebook, but his account is private. "Drat," she mutters. Maddie decides not to friend him tonight. That'd be too desperate. She searches through his Instagram instead. It's public. A few minutes in she's completely disappointed. The guy's got more pictures of tractors, trucks, and cows than she cares to count. "Where's all the chicks," she wonders out loud. "He's been kissin' someone." She scrolls and scrolls. Nothing. No girls. *He must be like a closet playboy.* She thinks. *I bet he doesn't post a picture of all the girls he dates because he doesn't want them to know about each other. Maybe he's a player. Maybe he has a girlfriend right now.*

"It was just a kiss and a stupid freaking bet at that. I don't think he has a girlfriend, though. Mason may be a lot of things, but he's not a cheater. Not every guy is like Jeff." She rolls her eyes. "Shoot. Mason has me talking to myself like a crazy woman." She hugs herself and wonders how she let six years go by without talking to the one guy who meant everything to her.

Maddie closes her eyes and tries to ignore the parts of her that want to head right back to the bar and give kissing Mason another go. She sighs out loud and decides all this craziness has to do with her feelings over their friendship that ended so abruptly. *Six years is a long time to be separated from the guy who used to be my other half. I don't have too many childhood memories without Mason in them. He was always by my side, not so much my knight in shining armor, more like my emotional support, or rather a constant reminder that I had emotions. I was the tomboy, and he was the sensitive gay best friend, except he wasn't gay, a fact he reminded me of way too well tonight. Ugh. Why did that kiss have to be so stinking hot and why can't I get it out of my mind?* She pinches herself. "I'm not drunk now, so what's my excuse for thinking about Mason and how hot he made me and how much I want to kiss him again," she whispers and then continues.

"I'm definitely not going to kiss him again. That would not be wise. I'm only here for the summer. That's not that long and flings just aren't my thing. Surely the two of us can stay away from each other. If I stay as busy as I intend to I won't have time to think about Mason and his many marriage prospects I'm sure his busybody mother has lined up for him, excluding me, the last person she'd want her precious baby boy to marry. We may as well be Romeo and Juliet. That's how long and deep this dam of bitterness and pain runs that sits between us is. Dill pickles and French fries don't go together." She giggles to herself. "But they kind of do."

She lays back on the bed twirling her hair and entertaining the thought of walking into Mason's house as his girlfriend. *His mom would probably have a coronary.* Her heart pinches a little, knowing it's impossible for them to be together. She wonders what that means and why she's thinking about them as if they are together especially since she already decided they wouldn't be.

She shakes her head and whispers, "Maddie. Shut your imagination down. It's after midnight. You need to go to sleep."

———

The back door rattles, Someone's coming in. They're creepin' down the stairs. Maddie trembles with anticipation even though she has pretty strong suspicions of who's comin'. She can't help but notice ever since their kiss at the bar it's like they're magnetized, just like when they were kids. The only difference is this time Mason makes her think of procreation, not recreation. She knows she's got it bad.

He sits down on the edge of the bed and sniffs the air.

Maddie guesses he's smelling perfume—her perfume. Maddie hears him moving. He's likely getting undressed. Then she hears him chuckling to himself.

She feels like she should say something to let him know she's there. Anything. But she's frozen and more than a little curious. Doesn't he know she's there? She moves up against the side wall. Part of her wants to run. The other part of her, the part that can never forget the smell of Mason French—a little bit of sweat, dirt, and freshly mowed lawn, can't wait to see what happens next. He plops down beside her. His breath sneaks across the bed and hits her full in the face. She wrinkles her nose. His breath smells like he ate a White Claw popsicle.

She closes her eyes tight and lays still as a board. She doesn't want to be caught staring. She focuses on breathing normal, like she's sleeping. His arm bumps into her and he startles. His hand roams over her front and she slaps it away. "Watch it, Mason," she shout whispers.

"Ah, Maddie Dill. I thought that was you," he whispers back, as if it's the most normal thing to lie down beside her. A second later, he's all up against her. She catches another whiff of their childhood. Her smile creeps out and betrays her. On some level, she knew tonight might end up like this. It was only a matter of time. She's thankful for the dark and she's glad Mason is drunk. She knows the only way she'll survive tonight is knowing she's probably the only one who will remember anything tomorrow.

His arm goes around her waist and starts climbing. She grabs hold of him and holds his hand tight to her waist. His hand relaxes. He breathes softly on her neck. Maddie can't help but notice how right it all feels. "I'm finally home," is the last thing he says before falling fast asleep.

Her eyes fly open at his words. She wills herself to calm down and go to sleep, but how can she? She can't believe his admission or how hard it hit her like a bullet between the eyes. She can't believe she was with Jeff for three years. They were about to be married, even. He never came close to saying anything like that. Sure, he said "I love you" enough times, the three words every girl wants to hear, but somehow the three words Mason just said mean so much more.

Five

Mason wakes to a hand on his boxer shorts. He holds both his hands in front of him to be sure he isn't imagining things. His eyes fly southward. A grin breaks out on his face. "Nope. That's not my hand," he whispers.

He looks over at Maddie Dill whose eyes are open, he thinks, but he can't be entirely sure. Her big brown eyes roll around just enough to be creepy. Even so, there's no denying she's beautiful. He startles as she sleep-stares back at him. Her hooded eyes grow darker, which he didn't think was possible. He feels turned inside out. Some things never change. He can't tell if she's trying to hide her desire or her dislike. He decides to go with desire. He moves as little as possible. Kind of. He snags his phone to snap a pic because he can hardly believe where he is or who is lying next to him, but his grown-up self decides against it. He settles for poking Maddie's forehead instead. "Maddie. Care to take your hand off my pants," he teases.

Her half-asleep eyes fly wide open. She jerks her hand away from Mason like he's diseased. He's almost hurt, but he's too satisfied knowing Maddie was the one being handsy. "I was asleep. As if." Mason starts at her teenage reference to *Clueless*.

"You still quoting that idiotic movie," he accuses.

She gives him a shove. "Whatever. Don't pretend you didn't like it. We watched it enough times."

He swallows hard. "C'mon, Maddie. It was *your* favorite movie, and I didn't want to tell you no."

She blushes. "Whatever. Don't pretend you weren't drooling over those plaid skirts and tight sweaters." She coughs. "You were a thirteen-year-old boy."

He snorts. "Think what you want. I'd fall for braids, overalls, and cowgirl boots any day." He stops talking a little too late. She flushes at the description of her go-to farmgirl outfit she wore when every other girl seemed to be busy making some sort of fashion statement.

He shifts a little bit. "I guess *Clueless* wasn't all that bad. It was the only thing that could make you smile that year. Remember?"

She blinks. "Yeah, I remember. That was the year I almost lost my brother, Billy."

He stares up at the ceiling. "Yep. I still can't believe the one thing that saved him was that idiot, Larry, who found him and dragged him out of the water before he drowned."

She glances over at Mason. "I still don't know why Billy was driving out south of town that night on that dirt road before he went off the side of the bridge that crosses over the river. His car went right down the embankment and into the water where it flipped on its top before it sank."

He sighs. "Aw, well. At least he was found. If you think about it, I guess Billy kind of bailed Larry out, or at least made him a little more honorable than the low-down cheat he'd been most of his life. I'd hate to think of what would have happened if Larry hadn't seen the whole thing." He grins a little bit. "The only question that night was which bored housewife walked her trampy butt home after leaving Larry's car. The identity of the mysterious caller who called the dispatch remains a mystery to this day."

"So what?" She frowns. "The important thing is that Billy came home."

He's annoyed, but he can't figure out why. "That's right.

Billy came home. No DUI. No ticket. Just a welcome-home party in his honor and your campaign to 'Block the Bridges'."

She thumps his sternum. "So what?"

He shrugs his shoulders. "Some people would say if someone's dumb enough to drive drunk, just let them drive off the side of a bridge."

She wipes a tear from her eyes. "You're saying I should have done nothing when my brother made a mistake that almost killed him?"

He knows he's being petty and ridiculous, but he can't stop. "I'm just saying it's awful interesting that you can forgive Billy for driving drunk, but you wouldn't forgive me for such a small thing as trying to kiss you."

She crosses her arms on her chest and takes a deep breath. "It's been six years, Mason French. Build a bridge and get over it."

"I swear your head is about as thick as those stupid three-foot retaining walls you had put up all over town because of your brother's bad decision," he grumps.

Her face is full of confusion as he side-eyes her. "I'm not the only hard-headed person here, and what do my safety walls have to do with any of whatever is between us?"

His whole body stiffens. "All I'm sayin' is those walls aren't the only place you left a permanent mark." He swallows hard. "And don't tell me to get over it. I was sixteen-years-old when you walked away. We'd talked to each other every day for twelve years and then all of a sudden you wouldn't say one word to me." He stares her down. "How could you do that? Did our friendship mean so little to you?"

She stares at the ceiling. "Don't go pretendin' you're the only one who had any feelin's, Mason." She growls in her don't-mess-with-me voice that would always shut him up in the past, but he's not taking it now.

He shifts from his back to his side. He leans over her and gets in her space. She turns away and stares off to the side at the wall. "Look at me, Maddie," he orders.

She turns back. Her big brown eyes look up into his grey ones. "What."

"What are your feelings for me?" he asks.

She grabs him by the tee shirt and yanks him toward her. "Right now, you're bein' a real pain in my ass," she growls as she glares up at him. "I want you out of my bed, Mason French."

He smirks down at her as his lips hover over hers. "You can say what you want, but we both know whose hands were where."

She lets go of his collar, sits up, shoves him, puts him in a side headlock, claps a hand over his lips, and turns to whisper in his ear. "Shut it, French Fry. Baby Novalee is sleepin' upstairs. The last thing I want is for Alex and Trint to know you're here with me."

There's a footstep on the stairs. Their eyes fly toward the sound. Alex appears halfway down the stairs as if she's been summoned. She stares at the two of them. Her eyes sparkle and shine. She claps her hands together and grins ear-to-ear. "I knew it. I soo knew it." Alex looks at them with triumph in her face. "Trint is payin' up, big time. We bet money on how long it would take for you two to get together. He basically said 'never', and I said, 'as soon as they see each other.'" Alex raises a victory fist in the air. "Ha. I was right."

As if cued the baby cries. Two circles slowly form on Alex's shirt. Mason looks away as Alex cups her front with her hands. "Dang it, I'm still not used to feeling like a leaky faucet." Alex turns around and flies back up the stairs.

Mason turns to Maddie. "Well, I guess our secret's out now."

She shoves him so hard with her feet that he hits the floor. She whips her bottom half back under the covers. She stares him down. "There's no secret to tell. Nothin' happened last night." Her mouth goes dry as another thought pops up. "How many bets were made about us last night? Was this right here another one?"

He stares right back at her. He knows there was only one bet, but he's not about to tell her that. He's still smarting from being rejected by Maddie again. He decides to let her think what she wants, which makes it way too easy to piss her off. "So what if it was? It doesn't mean I didn't want to be here with you."

She rolls over to face the wall. Her back is to him. "I'm so stupid. How did I not see any of this coming? It's like the ultimate prank to play on someone who's been pranking everyone else her whole life." She turns back to him and pats the bed beside her. "Climb back in here." Maddie's voice is all sexy and low, but he's not about to be fooled. She always has something up her sleeve.

"Why?" he demands.

"Don't you want to make good on your bet?"

He coughs. "Not like this, I don't."

She blinks and shoves the words he said last night from her mind. He was drunk so they didn't count, right? "Come on now. Don't be that way. Don't go pretendin' you have actual feelin's for me. If you did, you wouldn't have made any of this a bet," she reasons, but he can't tell if she's trying to convince herself or him.

He rolls his eyes. He wishes he'd kept his mouth shut because stupid things fly out of his mouth whenever he's around Maddie. "I'm not talking about the bet now. It's not a good time," he says with a sigh. "It was just something that slipped out over one too many beers, and then my pride took over and I ran with it a little too long. I gave you the money for the kiss."

She sniffs. "Yeah, and then you climbed right in my bed."

He slaps the floor which he sits on. "This isn't your bed. It belongs to my friends. I had no idea you were here, but I'm not sorry it happened. I'm not sorry for any of it." He sighs heavily. "I'm not going to pretend nothing happened between us because something did. This isn't over."

She wrinkles her nose. "We were both drunk. You mauled me. That's all that happened. There's nothin' between us." She hops up out of the covers in booty shorts that are barely there. He wills his mouth to stay shut. Her hands fly to the hem of her shortie tee shirt like she can somehow stretch another six inches out of the material. She clears her throat. "Anyway, I've got to get home. I'll see you around, I'm sure."

He shamelessly looks her over just to make her fidget, or at least that's what he tells himself. "Yep. You sure will," he confirms.

She frowns. "Get up off the floor. You look like an idiot. Don't go readin' too much into our kiss. There was hardly anythin' there. It was certainly nothin' to write home about. I've got a lot going on this summer and I don't need any complications." She studies him. "Do you hear what I'm sayin'?"

Maybe it's her confidence or the fact that it sounds like she's trying to convince the both of them, but he isn't done. "You're just as bitter as everyone says," he states as he stands up next to her. He waits for a comeback. She bites her lips like she's trying as hard as she can to hold it in, but she's like a bubble ready to pop so he keeps up his needling. "Don't you think you're a little young to be such a cold woman who's only chasing a career and has no time for any fun? I'd almost believe what everyone says about you if I hadn't kissed you last night. But I did and our kiss told me there's more to you than what's on the surface."

She blinks in annoyance. "Stop talkin'. Now is not the time for an argument." She turns up her nose. "And you don't know me like you think you do so don't pretend you know anything about my life."

He hurriedly throws the rest of his clothes on. He's eye-to-eye with Maddie Dill. He wonders why he still wants to kiss the crap out of her and her delicious little lips that are full-on sneering. He smirks down at her. "I intend to know you, Maddie." He leans in and hovers over her lips. "I intend to know you real well," he promises.

She makes a move on him, but he leans away. Her face colors with embarrassment. He chuckles. "You were totally chasing me just now."

"In your dreams, Mas-on French," she bites out. "That's the only place I'm chasin' you."

He winks in response. "Are you telling me you never dream of me 'cause I'm pretty sure we both know that's not true?"

Maddie blushes again and his heart soars. "You *wish* I had dreams about you," she responds, but it's seconds too late. Something in her voice betrays her and gives them both pause.

He backs away slowly, keeping his eye on her as he goes. "I won't wait another six years to see you again. I can promise you that," he says with a smile. He does a spin turn and walks out whistling. Mason knows one thing; Maddie Dill can't make him break his oath.

He turns back around to give her one last look. "You may have left Kentucky to go to some fancy college up North, but you're still a Southern girl at heart. That homegrown accent that you detest so much, pops right back out any time you're angry, hurt, or scared," he taunts.

"Shut up, Mason," she growls. "You don't have the first clue about what you're talkin'." Her words stop as fast as his smug grin flashes, blinding her. She clears her throat. "You don't know what you're talk-ing about," she enunciates slow and loud. "I did not go "up North" she puts in air quotes with her hands. "I went to KU. It's in Kansas."

"Ha," he proclaims. "Then you oughtta know Kansas was where the Civil War began. They were fighting against slavery. That makes them northern in my book," he says while throwing a hand on his hip.

Her brown eyes narrow. "Are you sayin' you're for slavery, Mason?"

He snorts. "You know darn well I am not," he declares. "I was merely making a point, a point on which you would agree with me if you weren't so dang stubborn. I'm out."

"Well, good riddance," she calls after his retreating form she wishes didn't look so good.

MYSTERY COUPLE

THANK GOODNESS FOR FAMILY!

The year was 1964 and the date was February 29th. It was a leap year! I had never met my future husband before that night. He was a guy my cousin knew. The night we met I guess we both decided to leap because we were pretty much inseparable after that. Five months later we were married. They say when you know, you know.

After we married, I worked as a legal secretary, and he worked for the county. Then in 1966, the draft came along, and my husband went into the Army Reserves. I became an army wife. We were married forty-four years, five months, and seven days. I still miss my husband every day. At times in our marriage, we were separated by war and patriotic duty.

My husband was an honorable man. He always came back to me and our children. That's love.

- Maddie Dill
The Daily Chase

Six

Maddie parks her mom's old car in the circle driveway before walking up the front steps. She plops down in a rocking chair on the porch to look out at the ducks in the pond in the distance. She wishes she could calm down just like she wishes she wasn't so annoyed. She buries her head in her hands. "What am I doing? I'm not in town two days and I end up in bed with Mason French," she grumbles.

"Did I just hear Mason French's name uttered on my porch?" Maddie's mom peeks out the front door with a smile. She holds two coffee cups. "Can I sit with you?"

She leans back in the rocking chair. "Sure, Mom."

Her mom is tall, blonde, and thin as a rail. Maddie reaches out and picks up the cup to take a sip. She lays her head back and smiles. "Man, I missed your coffee."

Her mom's head turns sideways in her rocker. Her bright blue eyes sparkle and shine as she pegs Maddie with an ornery grin. "How loud did Mason's mom scream when she caught you in his room this morning?"

Maddie giggles. "Mother, you are awful. That's not what happened at all. I wasn't in his bedroom."

"You weren't? But you just said you spent the night with him," her mother prompts.

Maddie feels her face heat up. "I did, but I didn't, okay? Nothing happened between us." She recalls their kisses. "Well, at least not that."

Her mom looks confused. "Are you telling me that the two of you spent the night in a hotel last night and didn't even have a little fun?"

Her jaw drops. "Are you tellin' me to sleep with Mason French? We're not even close to getting married." She takes Jeff's ring from her pocket and holds it up in the light. "It wasn't that long ago, and I was going to walk down the aisle with Jeff."

Her mom wrinkles her nose. "Yeah, well. Thank God that didn't happen."

She glances at her mother. "You never liked him. You hardly gave him a chance."

Her mom takes a long sip of coffee and stares out at the yard. "And now you know why." She sighs out loud. "Oh, Maddie girl. Just be glad you dodged a bullet with that one. He was definitely not good enough for you."

Maddie closes her eyes and leans back in the chair. "You'd say that about any guy I dated, Mom."

Her mom laughs. "And I'd probably be right. I'm your mother. That's my right." She taps a finger on her chair. "But I'd say Mason French comes awful close."

She chokes on the air. "For real? Doesn't his mom like hate you?"

"Possibly, but that's neither here nor there. All I'm saying is, if you married Mason French, it wouldn't be the worst thing. I really like him. I always have."

Maddie snorts. She can hardly believe her ears. "But what about the family feud that's gone on for generations?"

Her mom rolls her eyes. "That's old history. It has nothing to do with you and Mason." She takes a sip of coffee. "Besides, it has to end sometime. It's getting a bit ridiculous."

Maddie frowns again. "Whatever, Mom. All I know is, his mom can't stand you and you can't stand her." She giggles. "You two would eat each other's kidneys if you could."

Her mom groans. "Thanks for that disturbing imagery." She winks at her daughter. "Besides, I'm more of a gizzard girl myself."

She giggles. "And you wonder why I go straight for the jugular. Geez, Mom."

They sit there a while in silence. Maddie's head swims. Between this strange conversation with her mom and Mason's whispering in her ears she doesn't know what to think. "Change has to happen some time, Maddie. It's okay if you fall for Mason. That's all I'm saying," her mom adds, affirming Maddie's fears and confusion. Her mom is getting old.

Maddie shakes her head. "I don't understand how you could see through Jeff when I couldn't. What's wrong with my judgment?"

Her mom reaches over and takes her hand. "A mother always knows. That's just the way it is." She gives her a grin. "You'll know when you have your own someday."

Maddie groans and pulls her hand back. "You're just sayin' that. You didn't like Jeff because he wasn't Mason." She looks down at the sizable diamond ring in her hand. "His cheating was just icing on the cake."

"There's probably some truth in that." She tilts her head to the side. "What did Jeff think about Mason, or vice versa?"

She feels all weird inside. "I don't know. I never told either one of them about the other. They never met."

Her mom's smile disappears. Her gaze stills. "I see."

Maddie stands up and paces the front of the porch. "It's not a big deal. I hadn't talked to Mason for six years. I didn't even invite him to the wedding."

Her mom sighs again. "Oh, honey. Doesn't that tell you something was there?"

"Maybe, but it's not what you think. What it tells me is Mason and I shouldn't be around each other. We're like two sticks of dynamite. The only question is which one of us will blow first."

Her mom laughs out loud. "Well. What's wrong with having

a little excitement in life? It's kind of fun. Besides, that's right up your alley." Maddie's thoroughly annoyed with the satisfaction written all over her mom's face.

She frowns. "I've had enough of this nonsense just like I've had enough of Mason French." She gets up. "I'm going inside."

Seven

Maddie's phone goes off as she steps into the kitchen. She can't help but smile at Alex's Snap. Her baby's face is covered in off-white goo.

Alex: Hey, Maddie. What's up with you and Mason? You two are bananas, b-a-n-a-n-a-s, just like what's on Novalee's face.

Maddie giggles at the Snap.

Maddie: You're such a dork, Alex. I still can't believe you named your daughter after your favorite movie character.

Alex: Whatever, Maddie. Maybe I'm hoping she'll marry a librarian. We need at least one classy person in our family. Now stop avoiding the question. What's with you and Mason?

Maddie: Swear to secrecy, Alex Renee Snow?

Alex: Always, Maddie Carter Dill. Alex Snaps back.

Maddie: Truth: I can't believe I spent the night with Mason French, and I can't believe how bad my butterflies were going off this morning. My body betrays me every time I'm around him. What is it about him that sends me straight over the edge?

Maddie types away furiously. Her blood boils when Alex screenshots her words.

Screenshot me one more time, and I'm done talking to you, Alex.

Alex: Fine. I'm sorry. I can't read as fast as you. Seriously, calm down.

Maddie feels bad.

Maddie: I'm sorry. I just don't want this getting back to Mason. Got it?

Alex: Fine, but you're no fun. What good are all the feels if you don't act on them?

Maddie: Alex. I can't help how I feel, but I can help what I do, Maddie Snaps back.

Alex: I guess, but what's the point of having freaky feelings if you do nothing?

Maddie: Chillax, Alex. I just need some time to sort them out. That's all.

Alex: True that, but this summer will be over before you know it and then you'll be off to the big city. Chasing your dreams. And who knows when you'll see Mason or the rest of us again.

Maddie's heart sinks a little.

Maddie: Hey, don't hate on my dreams.

Alex sends her a hot air balloon pic.

Alex: No one's hating on you, Maddie. We're all hoping for you, but we're still your friends. We're still going to miss you when you go.

Maddie frowns.

Maddie: I miss you too, Alex. But I have to take a chance and it can't be on love. I tried that already and it ended badly.

Alex: That's 'cause you picked the wrong guy. They're not all like that.

Maddie's ears burn. This sounds too much like the conversation she just had with her mother, and she doesn't want go hear any more.

Maddie: I've got to go, Alex. I've got articles to write. And thinking to do.

Alex: Catch you later. Let me know if Mason shows up.

Maddie cringes at Alex's parting words. "Yeah, right," she whispers to herself. "Like he'd ever show up at my door."

She walks through the quiet kitchen lost in thought. She smiles to herself. *Everybody's at work. I guess I'd better get to it.*

Maddie logs on to the local newspaper site and scans the e-mails for more meet-cute stories for her to edit. "It's just my luck the first assignment I got was writing local 'how we met' stories for the couples around town. Just another reminder my love life is a big old failure." She mutters to Sully, her mom's beautiful Bernie who lays in the corner still as a rug.

Maddie's phone rings. She smiles when she sees it's her brother Billy calling. "Hey, what's up?"

"Not much. I had a minute and so I thought I'd call. I'm sorry I haven't been over since you got back to town, but things are busy on the farm. You know how that goes."

Maddie laughs. "Totally. I so don't miss those days." Maddie clears her throat. "How's Lisa? Still treatin' you better than you deserve?"

Billy laughs. "Ouch. Thanks for that sisterly affection."

Maddie smirks into the phone. "Anytime."

"So. What are you up to besides following Mom around?" Is it Maddie's imagination or did Billy's voice just crack a little?

"Didn't Mom tell you? I'm in charge of the meet-cute stories this year."

"What the heck is that?"

"You know, the ones Jeannette usually writes?"

"I really don't. I'm sorry."

Maddie clears her throat. "You know how Jeannette is huge on community and she loves getting everyone involved?"

"You say that like it's a bad thing," her brother teases.

"No, I didn't. I didn't mean that. I'm just explaining some-thing," Maddie all but yells at him. "You want to know or not?"

There's a long sigh on the other end. "Spit it out, Maddie. Geez," her brother says.

"I guess her eyes and ears aren't what they used to be or at least that's what she said when she called me up and asked/de-manded I be the next one to carry the torch."

Billy laughs. "She totally got you, and I didn't think that was possible."

Maddie groans. "She so didn't. I knew I was being played, okay? But who says no to a senior citizen? She's the woman who was my 4-H leader and taught me everything I know about livestock and proper protocol for model meetings," Maddie bristles.

"Okay, okay. Calm down already. Sheesh."

Maddie sighs. "As I was saying, Jeannette started a Valentine's Day tradition in the middle of August, and it's called half-Valentine's Day."

"That's weird," Billy interjects.

Maddie rolls her eyes. "I know, but it's tradition. I can't believe you don't know any of this."

Billy groans. "I don't know any of this because I'm not ninety-years-old. I've got better things to do than sit around reading the town newspaper. If I want to know what's going on, I head down to the Red Dog Saloon about once a month."

Maddie clears her throat. "Fine. But as I was saying, it's a special supper put on by the youth in our town. Leading up to it, the local paper features meet-cute articles from different couples in town anonymously. They are all numbered. At the dinner, each couple writes down who they think each article could be. Whoever has the most correct answers wins a basket full of gift certificates to local businesses, which is an awesome prize."

"That would be nice. Maybe I'll enter Lisa in it."

"That's a great idea. Thanks for your support. Anyway, this year I am said writer of all this romanticism which I'm not looking forward to, but it'll be nice to spend one last summer at home before I go off into the real world for good. And this internship is something I could put on my resume."

"So you gonna give me any hints on who you are writing about so I can like get a leg up on the competition?" Billy's voice is all hopeful.

"No, Billy. I am not. That wouldn't be fair at all, not to mention it'll look more than a little suspicious if you win when I'm the one writing the articles." Maddie taps her finger on the counter. "You'll just have to read them like everyone else does and do your best at guessing who they are."

Billy sighs. "Fine."

Maddie stares out the window. "Did you need anything?"

"Not really. I was just callin' to see how mom is doing."

Maddie thinks of their conversation on the porch. "She seemed pretty clear to me."

"Good. Well, I guess I'll talk to you later." Billy ends the call.

Her phone lights up again. Alex is back.

Alex: So, I forgot to say what I meant to say earlier.

Maddie can't take much more truth-telling this morning.

Maddie: Okay?

Alex: Thanks for saying goodbye, Maddie. I thought your momma raised you better.

Maddie blushes with shame.

Maddie: You're right. She did. I just had to get out of there.

Alex makes a purple emoji face.

Alex: Could it have something to do with your bedfellow?

Maddie giggles.

Maddie: That's one of the reasons I love you. You understand my love of strange, outdated words. To answer you—we're hardly bedfellows. Last night was a one-time thing.

Alex: So, something happened? Do tell! Emoji eggplant, eggplant. Maddie cringes at the emojis, feeling disgusted.

Maddie: No. Nothing happened. Calm your little horny heart down. I slept. He slept. That's it. I shoved him to the floor if you must know. That's how irritated I was to find him there.

That and the fact that Maddie's hand was on Mason's junk, which should have grossed her out but didn't. The last relationship they had was when Mason was her best friend. It's not normal to want to touch your best friend's junk. Maddie shakes her head to clear it.

Alex: Your irritation means you feel something for him. You can't ignore your feelings forever. I say go for it.

Maddie can't help but think she's heard these words today twice. What does it mean? There's no way her mom has been talking to Alex, is there?

Maddie: Whatever, Alex. We're practically the Hatfields and McCoys or the Montagues and the Capulets. That's how much our families hate each other. I don't see that changing anytime soon.

Alex: What better reason to follow your hearts and bring an end to the feud that's been going so long no one even knows what started it!

Maddie grins and wishes she had half the optimism of Alex. Then she rolls her eyes.

Maddie: I know what started it. Remember the genealogy project? I'm the one who found the answer. Mason's great-great-great-great grandpa stole my great-great-great-great grandpa's fiancée on the ship to America.

Alex does an emoji sigh.

Alex: Well, if that's even true that's a lot of greats and this generation needs to get over it. What sense does it make to carry a grudge between two people who are long gone? The Mayflower is ancient history.

Alex has a valid point but Maddie's not about to admit it.

Maddie: Alex, I know you love your matchmaking, but you need to leave the two of us alone. I'm going back to my job at the end of the summer and Mason's starting his. And that will be that.

FaceTime lights up Maddie's phone. It's still Alex, who apparently has more to say. Maddie wants to avoid speaking right now, but she's avoiding reading or writing happily ever after stories even more. Maddie opens it. "Yes?"

Alex's eyes are full of excitement. "I just heard from Trint that Mason was doin' some serious talking about you to Chad Merk after you left the bar last night."

Maddie groans. "I'm sure you're wrong. Mason and Merk the Jerk aren't even close to bein' friends."

Alex giggles. "Well, they are now. Apparently, Chad had quite the crush on you in school and that's why he was so mean to you."

Maddie's eyes narrow. "Now I know you're telling stories. That's so not true. Chad hated me and I hated him."

Alex just keeps going like she didn't hear Maddie. "It all makes sense now. Chad hated Mason because they both liked you. I can't believe we didn't figure this out sooner."

Maddie sighs. "First of all, you can't believe what you hear down at the bar. Everyone knows that. Most of what is said there are gross mis-exaggerations that might have a tiny bit of truth in them, if any, because people have nothing better to do with their ordinary lives except to make stuff up about their neighbors."

Alex does a huge eye roll. "Whatever. I got this information from a reliable source. Besides, I can't believe you of all people are questioning what people witness. Isn't that the very core of journalism?"

Maddie feels bad. "You make a valid point. I'm sorry if I hurt your feelings. All I'm saying is whatever Chad and Mason said or didn't say about me at the bar last night over a few too many beers really doesn't matter, because I have no intentions of starting anything up with Mason French. His feet are firmly planted in the soil here, the last place on earth I intend to settle down."

Alex snorts. "It'd be a cryin' shame if you ended up living around all your friends and family, the people who love and care about you. That'd just be the worst."

Maddie sets the phone down and digs through the fridge for something to make. "We talked about this earlier and you weren't so angry then."

Alex sighs. "I know. I'll try harder to be happy about you wanting to move away, but you know I don't like change." Maddie stands by her phone preparing the food. Alex walks out of the picture. She returns, carrying Novalee. Trint shows up in the corner. They're kissing. It's awkward, sweet, and gross at the same time. Maddie walks away from her phone and gets busy with the skillet.

Maddie clears her throat. "Besides, Alex; statistically speaking a small percentage of people settle down in the town they grew up in so I'm not the only one who wants to see the world." Maddie walks back to the phone.

Alex snorts. "We'll see about that." Alex whips out a nipple and Novalee latches on.

Maddie looks away, but not soon enough. "Next time, warn me before you bring out the horns."

Alex laughs. "Horns?"

Maddie raises her eyebrows. "Would you rather me call them udders?"

Alex shrugs. "Just call them areolas. That's what they are."

Maddie shudders. She can't believe Alex just said areola. Motherhood and nursing have definitely changed her best friend. "I'm just gonna go now. I'll talk to you later."

Alex shakes and shimmies just enough to get things moving. "Me and my girls say byee-eee."

Maddie laughs and turns off the phone.

Eight

Mason glances around in wonder and disbelief at the thought that he's literally standing at Maddie's backdoor, a place he's never been before because he was so worried about getting shot in his younger days. Mason glances around nervously, scanning the area for the end of a double-barreled shotgun. He knows his fears are ridiculous, but he can't seem to stop fidgeting. He rings the doorbell before he loses his nerve. He tries to think of a reason to be on Maddie's front porch step other than checking her out again and wishing she was his.

She opens the front door and yanks him inside. She jerks him into the kitchen and ducks down. "Stay away from my window. I don't want anyone seeing you here," she whispers, as if anyone can hear. He glances over at the big dog who might be more menacing if it wasn't sprawled out like an immovable rug that snores.

He fights the urge to laugh out loud. "My truck's outside in your driveway. I'd say it's a little late for that," he says with confidence he doesn't feel.

"Are you trying to get me kicked out of my family home before midnight tonight? You shouldn't be here," she hisses.

He plops down in a kitchen chair and looks around the room. "Hmm. There's no red walls or burning fire everywhere."

She makes a face at him. "Ha, ha. You're so funny."

He leans back in her kitchen chair. "That smells good. What you making?"

She raises an eyebrow. "If I give you some, will you leave?"

"May-be. It depends on how good it is."

Maddie grins and props one hand on a jutted hip. "Prepare to be devastated, French Fry. I make a killer omelette. You don't even know." She's all flirty faced with him for about half a second before she remembers who she's talking to. Humor slides off and her game face is back. Disappointment settles in his chest.

Mason thinks to himself that it doesn't matter. He knows what he saw, and he's determined to break down her walls. His mission is half complete and she doesn't even suspect a thing. "Thanks."

She turns her eggs with care in the big skillet. She turns back to him. "So, what's your visit really about?"

Mason shifts in his chair. "I came to bury the hatchet."

She almost falls over while she tries to ignore the fact that this is the third person today who's told her something along these lines. It's like the world is conspiring against her. "That's impossible and you know it."

His hand reaches for her, even though she's halfway across the room. He lays it back on the table, feeling foolish as he clutches at the air. "Nothing is impossible, Maddie, not if you believe in it." He taps the table. "Remember your building block project?"

She grins ear-to-ear. "Yes. I do. We just talked about it last night. That felt so good to put up all those safety walls." She glances at him out of the corner of her eye. "We made a great team." Her voice is full of resignation, like she hates to admit the truth.

"Was being partners with me so bad?" She drops a plate of omelette and hash browns on the table in front of him with a clatter. He jumps a little and looks up at her. "Whoa. How'd you get that hash in there so fast?"

Maddie's other hand moves over his plate and opens. Salt

and pepper fall over his eggs. She winks at him. "Just call me Tinkerbell of the kitchen. There's your pixie dust." She smirks and whips around to saunter to the coffee pot. He knows he could watch that walk all day long. She pours a cup of coffee and brings it to him. He feels like a king, and he must look it 'cause she leans down next to his ear and pinches his shoulder a little too hard in the process. "Don't go feelin' too special. My momma taught me to be hospitable. These southern habits are hard to kick."

He doesn't need any hot sauce for his omelette. Her warm breath creepin' down his neck has smoke comin' out his ears. He chokes a little and nudges her away with his elbow. "Back off." He growls. "I'm tryin' to enjoy my breakfast."

She giggles and walks away super-duper slow. If he didn't know better, he'd say she was swingin' that back porch swing just for him, and if she's not, it's still workin'. Maddie fills her plate and sets it down. She gets her coffee and leans over to get milk from the fridge. He groans. She shoots up straight as a pencil and whips around to give him a glare. His eyes fly to his plate and stay there. He focuses on eating.

She sits down at the table all red-faced while she salts her eggs. She closes her eyes to pray. He gets about a minute of reprieve before her eyes fly open. She pins him with her dark brown eyes. "So, what's your idea for burying the hatchet?"

His thoughts are all over the place. He's not following. "What do you mean?"

She sips her coffee. "If you really want change, you have to have a plan. You can't just tell our families to get over a feud that has divided them for at least four generations and expect it to happen."

He focuses on his omelette. It tastes amazing. He looks up at her. "What's your suggestion?"

"This wasn't my idea to begin with. You think of something."

He sips his coffee. He looks past Maddie to the cow calendar hanging on the wall and an idea slowly forms. "I've got it. What if we put a calf in a predicament that borders both of our family's lands?"

"How is messing with a cow going to fix our problem?" She stares at him like he's an idiot.

He sighs. "I'm saying we put an unmarked calf in a position that it's stuck and then we both call our grandfathers to come rescue it. Then we hover close by to see what they say to each other to see if any old grudges come up."

"That idea's not half bad." A hint of a smile forms on her lips. "They say nothing brings families closer faster than a crisis." She raises a finger. "And I think I know just the place to find an unbranded calf. I say we call Alex and Trint."

He considers this. "What makes you think the two of them will help us?"

She grins and nods. "Because Alex wants the two of us to... get together." She says the last part really fast and really quiet. "And she loves to play tricks that don't hurt anyone." She takes her plate to the sink and turns back to him. "And there's also her strange fascination with our family feud that's been passed on to yet another generation."

"I don't know what's so fascinating about a curse," he mutters.

She giggles. "It's hardly a curse. Nothing bad has happened to either of our families."

He stares her down. He can hardly believe his ears. "I beg to differ. The feud is the reason we have a field of hate between us, the reason I lost my best friend, the reason I didn't get lucky last night, and the reason I can't ask you out on a proper date right now." He blurts.

She blushes and looks down at her plate. "Let's just focus on our project, shall we?"

He takes another bite of omelette and tells himself to be happy to see the elusive Maddie Dill for project reasons starting with scouting the property line. "So we need to find the perfect place for our next shenanigan."

He looks up from his breakfast plate to catch her staring at his arms. Her eyes fly to his face. "I beg your pardon?"

"We have to find just the right place to hide the calf," he says.

She nods absent-mindedly. "Yep." She fiddles with the tips of her red hair. "I could come by on Timber and pick you up."

Once again, he feels clueless by something Maddie says. "What's Timber?"

She laughs out loud. "He's not a thing. Timber's my horse."

He raises a flirty eyebrow. "You and I are riding a horse together?"

"I can handle it if you can," she dares before sticking out her tongue.

He smirks to himself as he walks away from her to put his plate in the sink. He walked right into that one, but he doesn't mind. Not one bit. He sneaks looks at her while she sits at her kitchen table where they just had breakfast. Mostly in peace. "Lookin' forward to it," he says as he swaggers toward her front door when all he wants to do is go right back to her.

"Be here the same time tomorrow after everyone's gone to work," she demands from behind him. He pauses at her door. He wonders if it's his imagination or if he hears excitement in her voice. He holds in a grin as well as his thoughts. He knows Maddie would say there's nothing between them, but she's not right about everything.

He turns back to face her one more time. "I'll be here, Maddie Dill. You can count on me."

Nine

Maddie reads over the latest meet-cute again and again, but her mind can't settle. She can't believe Mason showed up at her back door and waltzed right into her kitchen and back into her life. Just like she can't believe she's not the least bit upset about it.

She shakes her head. Can it really be that easy to start up an old friendship? She searches her mind for negative thoughts of Mason. She's shocked to discover she can't remember any.

It seems the only Frenches her parents had an issue with were Mason's parents and his grandparents and his grandparents' parents, etc. Their tirade was constant and exhausting.

Maddie also recalls a different memory. It's one of her mother, the eternal optimist, who every once in a while would start in on her dad about the hate field and how it was just a shame no one planted anything there, to which he would always reply, "Margaret, is a little bit of gardening worth the price you'll have to pay if you break the rules set in place long before you were born?"

She frowns to herself as she remembers the bare patch of land that sits between her family's property and Mason's, court-ordered to be left alone by some bitter French a few generations back. She always thought it was weird that it was left alone because really, who's going to know or care if someone broke the rules? And besides, what's a stuffy lawyer sitting in his starched shirt and strangling necktie in his office behind mounds of paperwork going to care if someone plants a bean-field in there or not? It's not his business to know what they're doing in their fields.

She steps away from the open laptop to clean up the kitchen. She glances at her watch. She's watching the time because Joe down at the newspaper's going to be on her butt if she doesn't get moving on her stories even though she's already done two. She snaps the rubber band against her wrist to calm her rising anxiety. "I've got to stop procrastinating. Then I wouldn't get so freaked out."

She rushes out the door and down to Joe's office. She sits at his desk waiting to be admonished for her tardiness, but Joe doesn't show. After waiting ten minutes Maddie gets annoyed. She heads down the block to the Chamber of Commerce to visit Kelly and Jen. Maybe they'll give her some feedback on her arti-cles. They're always helpful with community projects.

Maddie rushes through the screen door. Kelly's daughter, Sophie, moves around the room in her oversized summer sweater and silver glitter boots. "Hey, Sophie. I love your style."

Sophie smiles back at Maddie. "Thanks."

Maddie scans the room. "Seriously. Those are killer boots. Is your mom in?"

Sophie nods. "Yep. She's in the back room. You can go on in. She's having her morning coffee. She should be half-human by now."

Maddie runs to the back and peeks in the side room. Kelly sits at the table fanning through brochures. "Hey, Maddie." Kelly's big brown eyes peer over the fanned pamphlets in front of her face like a hand of poker. "So these are my choices for the summer festival brochure. I'm trying to figure out which one will drum up the most business. We really need to bring the crowds in this year. We've had a few slower summers. These are just the demos. I'm trying to choose the best one. Do you have time to take a look?"

Maddie sits down in a chair and taps on the table. "Sure. Let me think about that. Say, I'm writing the half-Valentine stories this summer and I'm trying to think of a way to get more people to come to me, so I don't have the awkward job of tracking them down and begging for people to contribute if they don't want to. I got a few, but I need some more." She snatches up a pen and continues her tapping as her eyes fly over the demos. "Do you think a flyer on the bulletin board downtown would work? What if I put some up in the local businesses and restaurants?"

Kelly smiles. "That's a good start. You might get more input than you want, but it's a sound idea." She sips her coffee and raises her eyebrows as she sets it back down. "I just love reading those meet-cutes. They're just so sweet."

Maddie cringes a little inside at her friend's nostalgic tone. "Yeah, sweet like a toothache."

Kelly taps her pen on the table. "Gi-rl. Stop being so cynical. What is life if you have no one to share it with?"

"Being alone isn't so bad. I can go where I want, when I want, and do what I want." Maddie shrugs. "I don't have to answer to anyone."

Kelly snorts. "That may be true, but no one answers you back either."

"Excuse me?"

"How long can you have a one-sided conversation before you get tired of what it says back to you, which is pretty much nothing." Kelly stares Maddie down.

"I don't know." Kelly's words make Maddie itch. "All I'm saying is I'm in no hurry to settle down." She coughs. "I mean, I thought I was, but it turns out he was an idiot." Maddie's voice is quiet.

Kelly frowns at her. "So you found a toad. It's not a big deal. Most of us have done it at least once. "

"Yeah, I guess." Maddie stares at the wall. "Thank goodness I didn't marry him."

Kelly gives her an ornery grin. "That's true. No one wants kids covered in warts."

"Gross." Maddie groans and leans back in her chair. "Well, all things considered, I'm glad I didn't get married." She fidgets in her chair. "I mean, that's the last thing I need to be doing right now. I'm just starting my career. The timing is all wrong. You know?"

"Maddie Dill. You just jinxed yourself and you don't even know it."

Maddie shivers at the thought. Mason's face flies into her head, unbidden. "Whatever. You're just razzing me."

"Darn right I am." Kelly tilts her head to the side. "I hear you and French Fry spent the night together last night."

Maddie rolls her eyes. "So it's all over town, huh? Terrific."

"You know how it is when you live in a town of 2,000 nosy neighbors. People got nothin' better to do than pass out gossip like it's candy." Kelly winks at Maddie. "But you lay a kiss on Mason like you did down at the Red Dog Saloon, you know people's tongues will be a waggin', especially since your families hate each other and all."

Maddie's back is up. "I never said I hated Mason. And he laid that kiss on me."

Kelly laughs. "I know you don't." She winks at Maddie again. "You forget I was your teacher in elementary school. The way you two ran around together, nothing would separate you short of a lightning strike." Kelly pats her chest. "It did my heart good the way you stood up for him." She laughs again. "That boy sure could make moon eyes at you. I never seen anyone have it so bad."

Maddie blushes. "I think you're exaggerating just a little."

Kelly shakes her head. "Nope. I know what I saw. That boy was plum gone on you. After what happened last night, I'd say not much has changed."

Maddie's stomach flips a little when she thinks of his kiss. "Mason's not crushing on me anymore. He may have thought I was something special when we were young, but that was before he went off to college to meet a bunch more girls. I bet he's got a girl waiting for him. That kiss was just a bet." Her voice drops off with her last sentence. Her chest tightens at the thought. She jumps out of her chair.

Kelly slaps the table. Maddie glances over at her in surprise.

Kelly looks ticked. "Don't be so hard on him. He's not the type to play around. Just because you're not ready to face your feelings doesn't mean he's a tool."

"That's a little harsh," Maddie argues. "Would you like it if some guy kissed you over a bet?"

"Is it? I think you're being awfully hard on a guy who's just trying to get to know you better. Trust me, Mason has no ulterior motive. He's not that kind of guy." Kelly gives her a wink. "And if the guy was a good kisser, I don't think I'd mind being a bet."

Maddie refuses to feel bad. She's about done with hearing everyone singing Mason's praises. "Alright, fine. I hear you. Everyone loves Mason. He's the best."

Kelly shakes her head back and forth. "No, miss snarky pants. I don't think you are hearin' me, but that's alright. Actions speak louder than words. You just wait. Mason isn't one for sittin' around and doin' nothing. I just hope you're smart enough not to pass on a good guy."

"Well, thanks for the advice. I'm just gonna go work on my flyer." Maddie skips down to the other end. She drops the handful of brochures and fans through them. The climbing tree by the hate fence with a sunset behind it catches her eye. Memories of sitting in the branches with Mason and talking about their dreams about how they were going to uncover the great mystery behind the feud flood her. They wanted to know the secret so badly. Then when it came out, she got so mad at him. Even though she doesn't know what she would do differently, she wishes she could turn back time.

"What's on your mind girl, 'cause I can see those wheels turning." Kelly's quizzical words are like a key turning a lock.

Maddie plops down in her chair. "I remember the day I found out that it was his family who wronged mine. I was so angry with him even though it made no sense. It wasn't his fault his ancestors were fiancée stealers. I remember being angry with him for changing on me. When I found out about the ship story I snapped. Thinking about all of it now I see that it was just bad timing."

"Bad timing how," Kelly prompts.

Maddie shrugs. "I don't know. By that time, he'd already tried to kiss me at the bonfire. After that I didn't know how to act around him. We'd been the best of friends, but he went and ruined it by trying to make a move on me. I guess I wasn't expecting any of it. When he tried to kiss me, it freaked me out."

Kelly nods her head in understanding. "I hear what you are saying. I'm sure all of that is true, but you know you weren't the only one whose feelings were hurt."

Maddie stares at the table. "No. I suppose not." She shakes off the memories as her finger rests on the tree in the picture. "Sometimes I wish things were as simple as they used to be is all." She taps the fence on the brochure and smiles as she slides it toward Kelly. "This one has my vote."

Kelly studies the dreamy look on Maddie's face. "I can tell there's a story there, but I won't pry anymore." She looks at the brochures again. "We might be a small town and not what you're looking for but sometimes what we're looking for isn't what's best for us."

Maddie stands up out of her chair. She feels stunned. She thinks she might have had a revelation, but she's not sure. She looks Kelly in the eye. "You talk like you're a minister's daughter or something," she teases as she tries to lighten the mood.

Kelly laughs out loud. "That may be, but I speak the truth."

Maddie waves at her friend before turning back around to walk out. "That's what I'm afraid of," she mutters to herself.

MYSTERY COUPLE

CAN YOU CHECK
MY PIPES, PLEASE?

I met my future husband when I was a college student at a state college. I lived in an apartment building. He was the handsome maintenance man who hid beneath a cowboy hat. It wasn't long and my apartment seemed to have more problems than any of the other renters. Although I had my eye on him, either I was seeing someone, or he was. Eventually, fate stepped in and we were both single at the same time. We went on our first date. It was just as special as I thought it would be. Once we started dating, it was like a whirlwind romance that scared us both, and so we took a break.

A few months went by. Although we weren't dating, we still ran into each other quite often at the local cowboy bar. The connection was undeniable. We both had our songs we would play on the jukebox to let the other know we were at the bar and ready to dance. During that time, it was so hard for me to dance with him because I wasn't sure if he would come back to me or if I should make the first move. Then one night he showed up at my friend's apartment and told me he loved me. It was the perfect new beginning. Now we are married, and he'll always be my dance partner!

- Maddie Dill
The Daily Chase

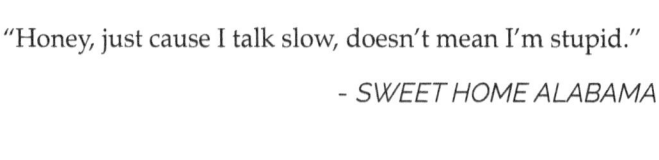

"Honey, just cause I talk slow, doesn't mean I'm stupid."

- *SWEET HOME ALABAMA*

Ten

Mason drives down Maddie's road feeling sneaky when her mom comes flying by in her brand-new silver Ranger. He ducks instinctively and finds himself about halfway in the ditch in his efforts to go unnoticed. He takes his foot off the gas and grips the steering wheel as he waits for his truck to right itself. He slowly returns to the gravel road.

"I'm such an idiot," he mutters. *If she's going to see me, she's going to see me. Besides, there's lots of other places I could be going—I just happen to be on this road.* He reaches out and turns up the radio. He rolls down the windows, chokes on the dust, and rolls them back up again as he tries to relax while listening to Merle Haggard singing *Rainbow Stew*.

"Maddie Dill, you'd better be worth all this trouble," he says as he pets Bambi, his dad's newest pride-and-joy hunting dog that he's been hauling around ever since Bambi showed up last Saturday unannounced. He shakes his head. "Bambi, you'd better not be the reason my mom goes over the edge." He takes in her tri-colored coat along with all of her speckles and her sad, dark eyes. "You sure are a pretty thing." Bambi turns away from him to look out the window once more. He chuckles to himself. "Ain't it just like a woman to give me the silent treatment when I'm just tryin' to be nice."

He drives up Maddie's drive. He takes a deep breath. "It's just a horse ride. Calm down," he mutters to himself as he climbs out of the cab and walks up Maddie's front steps to knock on her door. He raises his hand to grab the knocker when something moves in the corner of his eye. He turns to see her sitting atop a horse.

She grins from ear to ear. "Ready to go, cowboy?"

He tips his baseball hat a little. "I'm ready if you are." He gestures toward Bambi who sits by his side. "This is Bambi, my father's latest purchase, but he hasn't told my mother yet."

She stares at the dog. "I bet she cost your dad a pretty penny. That's one fine-lookin' huntin' dog."

He chuckles. "I forget. You always did know your animals better than me."

She rolls her eyes. "I grew up on a farm just like you. My years spent in 4-H at the dog shows taught me a thing or two. I know how to judge an animal."

"Much better than a fiancé, that's for sure," he mutters under his breath.

She gasps just enough for him to know what she heard. "You ready to go home now? We can call the whole thing off."

He coughs. "No."

"Then keep your mouth shut about Jeff," she demands as she stares him down. "You don't know anything about him."

He looks right back at her. "I know that he lost you." He steps up to the edge of the porch to wait. "Only a fool would do that."

She nudges her horse forward with her knees and makes a clicking sound. "Let's go then." Her horse walks forward a little. She tugs on the reins. "Easy, Timber," Maddie whispers soft and low. The quarter-horse comes to a stop. Mason hauls himself up behind her. His hands settle on her hips. He grips just a little to test the waters. She coughs and nudges at his hands with her elbows. "What're you doing?" Her voice is all squeaky. Satisfaction fills Mason who doesn't loosen his grip.

He sits closer to her and rests his chin on her shoulder. "I gotta hang on somewhere. I don't want to fall off."

She clicks her mouth again. "Come on, Timber. Let's walk." Timber is a decent-sized horse and there's plenty of room, but Mason remains snuggled up to her backside.

They ride in silence for a little while, but he doesn't do quiet. "Can I ask you a question?"

"Yeah." Her tone is even but he knows for a fact she can get riled real fast.

"I, um, well, I never could figure out why you got so pissy with me after you found out about my ancestors stealing one of your ancestor's fiancées."

She sniffs. "It's a big deal, that's why. What kind of person steals another person's fiancée?"

He knows he's making her mad, but he can't help it. "At least he did it before she was married."

She snorts. "He broke up a wedding. How does that make it better?"

Mason knows he's probably wrong, but he can't stop, because he also knows if he had known Maddie was engaged, he'd like to think he would have done something to stop her from getting married or at least told her how he felt. "Maybe it was bad timing. I mean, think about it. They were stuck on a ship for who knows how long and back then people didn't wait long before they married, and once a person is married, that's it. So he had all these feelings and he needed to tell her, and so he did. It's not his fault she left one guy for another."

She leans forward a little in her seat. "If your ancestor hadn't chased her, she never would have left my ancestor." Her voice is all self-righteous and Mason supposes she's right, but he's not convinced. Besides, it's just too much fun making her angry.

"All I'm saying is you don't know the whole story because you weren't there. They're the only ones who know the whole story, and they're both dead." He clears his throat. "Maybe your ancestor was dying or not well."

She turns to face him with narrowed eyes. "You're telling me if she married him to take care of him because he was sick that would be the wrong thing to do?"

He stares into her brown eyes. He's known her eyes all his

64

life, but somehow, they look different. Mason feels like he's drowning. "I'm saying a person should marry for love, not obligation."

She whips her head around again. "Well, I doubt my ancestor was sickly or dying. I bet as soon as that ship docked there was a duel."

"O-kay." He laughs out loud and rolls his eyes behind her head. "You just can't fathom anyone in your family being a coward. Is that what you are saying? It seems like you're giving some guy in the past an awful lot of credit just because he's family."

Her shoulders tense up. He fears he may have gone too far. "That's what family does. We give each other the benefit of the doubt."

"But not best friends," Mason mutters under his breath.

"What's that?" Her tone is sharp as a tack.

He knows he should quit while he's still on the back of a horse, but he makes another jab. "Or maybe your ancestor was not a nice guy, and my ancestor knew it and so he thought he was rescuing her from a terrible marriage."

She shakes her head back and forth and takes a couple of deep breaths. "I've half a mind to dump you on your stubborn butt right here. You don't know if any of what you are saying is true. You're just arguing to be arguing."

He laughs out loud again. "You going to tell me you never argue just for the sake of arguing? 'Cause we both know that's not true." Timber comes to a stop. She whips her feet around and hops off Timber. "What are you doing now?" he asks.

She looks up at him like he doesn't have a clue. "I'm wading in the creek bed. I need to cool off." She plops down on a rock and whips off her boots and socks. Mason's almost recovered from the sight of her pale pink toenails that shouldn't be turning him inside out when she whips off her shirt. He tries to look away from her light blue excuse for a swimsuit, but he can't. There's so much pale skin. As far as he's concerned, she's flawless. She puts a hand on her hip. "What you starin' at, French Fry? Haven't you ever seen a bikini top before?"

He looks away and heads toward the other end of the creek bed. He has one boot in the water before he realizes where he's at. He hops onto a little patch of grass and whips his boots and socks off. He tosses his hat to the ground before he whips off his tee shirt and steps into the creek. He tries not to cringe as crawdads crawl over his toes. "I hate crawdads. I hate them so much."

A splash of cold water hits his back. He whips around to see her standing behind him. Her eyes sparkle with orneriness. He doesn't think twice when he kicks water right back at her. It doesn't take long and they're both bent over, tossing cupped water at each other. She lunges at him, grabs a foot, and yanks. He can't believe he forgot she was a hardcore wrestler. He ends up on his butt in the shallow creek. She laughs so hard. He can't let her get away with that. He grabs her by the knees and takes her down. She ends up sitting across his thighs. The creek water is chilly, but having Maddie this close heats him through from his toes to his nose. He takes in her sun-kissed, freckled, turned-up nose. "Maddie Dill, what am I going to do with you?"

She bites her lip. Her solemn dark brown eyes stare right back into his. He hides his grin. Maddie never could look away. "I don't know," she says in a voice so quiet and unlike her it throws him.

He reacts on instinct and tips her off his lap backwards. She lands in the water. By the look of surprise on her face, he would guess ice-cold water just went down her shorts. Her pale face turns beet red. She splashes him like crazy until he's covered with water from head to foot too. As fast as she splashes him, she stops. Maddie stares at Mason like she's seeing him for the first time. She gets to her feet and looks down at him before her eyes cut to the side. "The fiancée on the boat didn't marry either of them. She found someone else." She looks at him again. "We were barely sixteen. I didn't expect you to try and kiss me. I wasn't ready for that, and I didn't want to lose our friendship. You were my best friend. I felt like you betrayed me." She steps onto the grass and puts her back to him to cover her embarrassment.

Her admission does little to soothe his wounded pride and old hurts. He takes a deep breath and tries to calm down. "So you'd rather lose your best friend instead of just talk to me about it?"

She shrugs. "It was almost seven years ago now. Let it go." She tugs on her boots and throws her shirt back on. "I have."

Her voice is all cool and nonchalant. He doesn't know what to think. Is she trying to convince him she has no feelings, or herself? "Whatever, Maddie. I know you felt something when we kissed down at the bar the other night. It wasn't all one-sided."

Her cheeks flush pink like they do any time she gets mad or overly excited. "Whatever. You were three sheets to the wind. I doubt you remember anything correctly."

If Maddie thinks her cruel words will push Mason away, she's mistaken. He jumps up and walks toward her. "You want me to prove you felt something? Are you challenging my word?"

She stomps away from him in a hurry. "That's not what I said at all. You're crazy." She walks at a faster pace. She scans the area as she goes. "Let's just find a place to hide the heifer." She disappears behind a tree. He rushes after her. Just like always, she's one step ahead.

He spots her standing off the path. "Here. I found it."

He makes a face at the smooth ground. "There's no hole there. Where are you going to hide a whole calf?"

She stomps on the dirt and digs in with the toe of her boot. The earth crumbles and gives way. "The water seeps into here and it makes the dirt super soft. It wouldn't take long at all to dig a hole here to put a heifer in." She taps her chin. "All I need is a shovel, a rope, and a pole."

He is more than a little confused. "What are you thinking?"

She rolls her eyes and holds up a finger. "The shovel is for digging." She holds up a second finger. "The pole is for an anchor." She holds up a third finger. "The rope is to tie to the pole to lower yourself and the heifer into the hole."

He can't believe she's being so obvious. "If you set all that up, don't you think our grandpas will know this was planned?"

"Does it matter?" She taps her booted toe. "Besides, maybe if they see what they can do together they will rethink their stupid feud."

He walks slowly toward her. "I think you're on to something. I wonder what would happen if our families spent more time trying to kiss and make up instead of fight." He's all up in her space by the time he stops talking. His thumb rests just beneath her chin.

"Mason," she whispers, gazing up at him.

. Maddie's lips beg to be kissed, so what's stopping him? He wants to kiss her in the light of day, but his pride still stings from being rejected by her too many times to count. And what about their precarious friendship hanging in the balance? He just got her back. He doesn't want to lose her again.

"Maddie," he whispers her name.

Her gaze is locked between his eyes and his lips. "Yeah."

He clears his throat. "I can't wait another six years to be your friend." He doesn't move an inch. "As bad as I want your kiss—I can practically taste it—I don't dare. Your friendship means too much to me." He feels defeated as he leaves the ball in her court. He pivots, spins, and waltzes away, giving her something to ponder.

Eleven

Maddie is shaken clean down to her toes when she discovers Mason French is the hottest tease she's ever known. He's got the anticipation game down. She frowns to herself as she watches him walk away. She thinks that's the last time she lets him camp out on her lips and then walks away, even though it's the second time he's done it. She's never had her pride sting so much. She shakes it off as she stares up at the trees. *Shoot, shoot, shoot,* she screams inside her head. She doesn't know how much more of this side of Mason she can take.

She's relieved to have an excuse to get away from Mason, if only for a little while. "So, I guess I'll just go back to grandpa's and grab the shovel and pole," she says as she glances in his direction. "You stayin' or goin'?" Mason frowns up at her. She swears it's like he can read her mind and she can't have that. "C'mon, French Fry. I'm gettin' old here." She tries a joke to lighten the tension between them.

"I think I'll just chill out here. The water feels pretty good," he said as he walks back into the creek bed.

"I'll be back soon," she says before she takes the reins, turns Timber around and takes off before he changes his mind. She gives him a few kicks. and Timber takes off at a run. She leans into him and lets him fly. The wind flies through her wet hair and chills her front, but she doesn't care. Another shiver runs through Maddie. She doesn't know if it's from the creek or Mason. Maddie's frustrated when she relives their conversation again in her mind. Where does he come off bringing up their drunken kiss? What's the point? And what was he talking about waiting six years to be her friend? Did their friendship ending hurt him as much as he carried on about it?

She thinks about Mason and his high school days. She remembers him keeping so busy it was like he didn't have time for her, much less time to spend pining over her. She speaks to the trees as she rides along. "I know he tried to kiss me, but it doesn't mean anything. I bet I was the first girl he felt comfortable with since we were such good friends. That had to be what it was." She stops talking for a few seconds. "But if it meant nothing to him then why is he still talking about it? And if it meant that much to him, why didn't he say something? Ugh. Mason French is a headache and a half."

She hops off to grab her stuff and keeps up her commentary. "Mason's so annoying. Here I thought we were back to being partners in crime and he has to go and bring up all the awkward history between us. I so don't need this right now," she grumbles as she wrestles with the tools and manages to maintain some sort of balance. It's a much slower walk back to Mason. She almost drops it all a few times, but somehow, she makes it. She giggles when she spies him sitting on the tree stump by the creek bed with his knees drawn to his chest. Only his feet hang over the edge.

"I see some things haven't changed. You always did hate all things nature and any kind of insect," she taunts.

She stops talking as his grey eyes meet hers. He looks serious. He hops off the tree stump and walks quickly to her side to grab the shovel as it slips down her leg. She tosses the pole off to the other side and hops down.

"Thank goodness. I thought my arms were going to give out trying to carry all that."

He snorts. "I'd offer to help you, but the day you ask for help..."

She bristles at his comment even though it's totally true. "What's wrong with being independent?"

He shrugs. "Nothing I guess, but we all need people. The day you stop needing others is the day you stop being human."

She snorts. "You talk about independence like it's a bad thing, but I don't know what's so bad about being self-reliant. Needy people are tiresome. They're real life-drainers."

He flinches. "That was way harsh, Dill Pickle. I can't believe how sour you sound. What stink bug crawled up your shorts?"

She refuses to feel bad. "Sometimes I like to do things for myself and by myself. What's so wrong with that?"

His frown slowly turns to a smirk. "Nothing. There's nothing wrong with any of that." He walks over and hands her the shovel. "Here. Have at it."

She stares back at him. "What do you mean?"

He grins at her. "I'm calling you on your crap. That's what it means. You say you don't need anyone's help. Fine. Go dig your own hole. I'll just sit here and watch since you say you don't need me."

She can hardly believe him or her telltale over-confidence and her stupid mouth. She glares at Mason. "You're really not going to help me?"

He throws up his hands as he settles back down on the stump. "The only thing worse than that reckless tongue of yours is your uncontrollable anger." He gives her a wink. "If you want my help, you're gonna have to ask."

She snatches the shovel from his hand. "Give me that shovel. I *will* do it myself. Just watch me." She stomps to the soft patch of dirt and ignores the sweat that drips down her back. She glances at Timber and notes the empty saddle. She feels foolish when she realizes she didn't bring a single bottle of water. She jams the shovel into the dirt and starts digging. She wonders if she has enough anger to dig a hole six feet deep.

MYSTERY COUPLE

SOMETIMES LOVE
IS A BLIND DATE

I was a shy small-town girl who felt plain and unnoticed. For the most part, I was okay with that. I was happy to be the ride-along third wheel of my best friend on all her dates. My best friend had a boyfriend and she wanted me to be happy too. So she was always setting me up on blind dates, but none of them took. One night my soon-to-be blind date cancelled last minute. I was all prepared to be the awkward third wheel like so many times before. My best friend wasn't satisfied with that. She persisted in searching for my special someone and we pulled up to her boyfriend's friend's house.

The minute I laid eyes on him and all his long blond hair, I was enamored. He was such a joker. He kept me in stitches all the way to the restaurant. After our wonderful meal, he paid for everyone's dinner. Although I was interested, I thought a sweet, funny, kind, and generous person like him would never go for me. I was so nervous being around him I got a stomachache. Even though we'd laughed together and even arm wrestled, I was pretty insecure about everything and was sure I'd never see him again.

He called me up the very next day. We made donuts in the snow and then we went out to eat. We've been married twenty-four years, and we've been doing donuts through life ever since.

- Maddie Dill
The Daily Chase

Twelve

M ason watches Maddie in disbelief as he looks at the time. It's been a good hour. He can't believe she is still going. He can't help but smile when he thinks of her hot temper, which has to be through the roof right now. He steals occasional glances at her, looking for any signs of a crack in the surface. If she hasn't reached her limit by now, he's not sure she will. He can't help but admire her grit. She can be as stubborn as the day is long. He knows it shouldn't make him hot, but it does. It's a bright sunny day and they've been out there for a while. He sits as still as possible in the heat, enjoying the occasional breeze. Her face grows pinker and pinker, but she keeps at her shoveling.

She removes her oversized gloves and wipes her hands on her shorts a few times. She winces. He feels bad about that, but he's determined not to get off this stump until she asks him to. He sits and waits impatiently. He holds his laughter in when he can't help but notice the longer he sits on the stump, the more heat she throws his way. He refuses to look her in the eye. Maddie's so hard-headed the only way to get through to her is to give her a dose of her own medicine. Besides, it's fun watching her literally dig her own hole. She's so good at it.

She clears her throat. He turns toward the sound to meet her fiery stare. "Did you say something?" he asks as he thinks she's making a face at his humorous tone, but he can't be sure.

She drops her shovel on the ground. "I'm gonna take a break. My hands are a little sore." She steps up out of the hole that's almost to her knees. He would be impressed if she weren't so short. He wants to help her so badly, but he's waiting for an invitation. He stretches his legs a little and wiggles his feet. He makes a big show of them almost touching the grass. Her eyebrows raise and her face relaxes. He pulls his feet back to rest them on the stump and resumes his sitting. Her face falls. It's priceless. She was never good at hiding her emotions. She gives him a look of resigned longing. It reminds him of his dog at home when she's begging for table food and doesn't get any. "I guess I'll get back to it then."

"Knock yourself out," he quips. This earns him a hotter-than-Hades glare. She wipes a tear from her eye. His jaw almost drops when he sees her bringing out the big guns. He'd feel worse if he didn't know her as well as he does. If she were any other girl, an apology would be in order, but she's not. She's Maddie Dill, which is why he knows she'll pull every Ace she's got before those hot lips of hers offer him an apology or a plea for help.

He looks on as she leans over with a groan and picks up the shovel. She puts the gloves on as slow as molasses. She starts digging again. Half of him wants to break her and the other half admires her grit, as his grandpa Steve would say. Another half hour drags by. He starts to feel a little ridiculous. The sun burns hot on his skin. He hasn't moved an inch. She's in the shade, but still. He steals more and more glances at her. She's moving about as slow as a turtle. Her sense of pride must be somewhat gone, as she stopped holding in her grunts from exertion at least twenty minutes ago. He thinks he really should say something, but he can't bring himself to do it. He'll show her she's not the only one who can give the silent treatment even if it is petty and childish.

He's looking around for Bambi when he hears a thud. "Seriously? Are you sleeping over there while I'm busting my tail?"

Something in her voice hits him dead center. He can hardly believe his ears. Is tough-as-nails Maddie really about to cry for real?

He studies her. "I wasn't sleeping."

She studies him right back. "You're going to make me say it aren't you?"

Hell, yeah, he thinks to himself. "I have no idea what you're talking about," he says in his best ever imitation of the many starring roles he's seen on too many episodes of COPS.

She sighs and jams her hands on her hips, then gives him her best mom stare down. He does his level best to look extremely bored with her adorable antics. She throws her head back and stares at the overhead leaves.

"Fine. Fine. Fine. I'll say it." She slowly drops her head to look at him again. "Mason French. Will you help me?" He smirks as those words pass from her lips as hard as a kidney stone.

He doesn't budge an inch. "Your request is missing one vital piece."

She groans. "Please," she bites out.

He slowly rises from the stump and struts toward her like she's just told him he can move mountains, because, in her world he kind of has. He grabs the shovel handle and steps into the hole beside her before he leans in. "You really gotta work on that delivery. If I was going by your tone alone, I'd have thought you told me to jump off a cliff."

She leans away to escape their intimate pose and takes a step back far enough to trip herself on the edge of the hole. She falls on her butt. He laughs out loud. She scoops a handful of dirt and chucks it on him. "Go to Hades, Mason French."

He winks at her. "Only if you'll come with me."

She picks herself up and dusts herself off. "I'm going to the creek bed."

He whips off his shirt and tosses it on the ground. He doesn't miss the very appreciative glance from Maddie, or the way it makes him feel. She stands there staring at him. "I thought you were going to the creek bed," he teases.

She steps back into the hole and plasters herself against him. "I thought I was." He doesn't think twice about their friendship or anything else. He can't when she's looking at him that way. He drops the shovel and wraps his arms around her to pull her closer. He doesn't know when the next opportunity will come or if he'll have one. He dives into their kiss that's hotter than the noonday sun. Her hands are on his neck and in his hair. His hands are everywhere. He can't get enough of her.

She moans just a little and they both are lost in the moment. He holds her even tighter and kisses her like there's no tomorrow. Eventually, he returns to himself. He feels more than a little awkward. His brain buzzes—what is he doing mauling Maddie in the middle of a field? He forces a little gentleness into the kiss. He wants her to know how much she means to him. He knows she can be all thorns sometimes, but her heart is as soft as a rose petal; at least it is to him. It hurts to do it but he backs off.

Her eyes are full of question and wonder when he pulls away. "I've got to finish digging this hole," he chokes out.

She stares at the ground. "Yeah, of course."

She takes a step out of the hole and walks toward the creek bed. She plops down in the water with a splash and leans back on her elbows in the grass. She wiggles her toes and moans just a little. He wants to moan too, so he pours all his frustration into his digging.

Thirteen

Maddie sits on the stump. She thinks it feels like too many hours have passed since she and Mason started taking turns with the stupid shovel. Even though the dirt is soft, she's rethinking this whole heifer idea. She walks toward him as he stands beside the hole. "What are you doing?"

He groans. "Trying to get excited about getting back in there."

"I hear ya. I can't feel my arms," she whines. He laughs and reaches out to give her arm a squeeze. "Son of a..."

He claps a hand over her mouth and coughs. "Just checkin' to be sure your arms are still attached." He flashes her a grin. "They are."

"You're so hilarious," she grumbles at him.

"Alright, alright. Calm down." He trails her arm a little with his thumb. She gets the shivers and takes her arm back. "I'm fine."

He grins over at her. "Hey. I'm just trying to help you." He looks all concerned. "I don't want you losing any feeling in your arms now."

She frowns a little. "Yeah. I know what kind of help you're offering."

He winks at her. "*You* kissed me under the shade tree. I didn't start it this time."

She blushes. "It was all the heat getting to me. That's all."

He laughs. "If you say so."

She glares back at him. "I've got plenty to say, French Fry."

He just laughs some more before he lays the shovel down and hops down in the hole. "Yeah, I'm sure you do." He leans against the wall of dirt. He's up to his shoulders. He grabs the shovel and digs for a while longer before he stops. "You think this is deep enough?"

She looks it over from up above. "I suppose."

He hauls himself up out of the hole. Every muscle in his arms strains. His back glistens with sweat. She can't look away. He looks over his shoulder with a knowing grin. "What you lookin' at?"

She rolls her eyes heavenward. "The sky."

He lays the shovel down and grabs the pole. He jams it into the ground and starts twisting it this way and that. It slowly sinks into the ground. He pulls on it next. It doesn't move much. "There. That oughtta do it."

She grins. "Yep. Now it's time to go get that heifer."

He frowns. "I'm about shot. I ain't carryin' no heifer all the way back here on the back of your horse."

She makes a face at him. "Duh. Neither am I. We'll just bring the ATV." She leads Timber to the stump to climb on but Mason shoves her out of the way and climbs on first. He sticks out his hand. "C'mon up."

She walks over and grabs his shirt laying by the hole and throws it at him. "You forgot something." He takes it and wipes off his face and shoves it in the saddle. She stares at all his skin. "You're not going to put your shirt on?"

He grins down at her. "It's too hot. You comin' or not?"

She hands the shovel up to him. "Take this."

She climbs back on the stump. He extends his hand again. She grabs his arm instead. It's slick with sweat. "Ew," she says as she lets go and wipes her hand on her shorts. She grabs his hand and somehow manages to climb on the back of Timber.

She tries to put space between them, but she feels like she's falling off. She scoots a little closer but sits up straight as her hands cling a little on his belt loops. She doesn't like that she likes having someone to hold onto.

"You ready yet?" Mason sounds annoyed.

"Yeah. I'm ready," she growls.

They start off at a walk. The shovel slides back and forth. He keeps stopping to right it. "Do me a favor and put your arms tighter around me so you can hold the shovel still, please."

She doesn't want to do that. She doesn't want to be all pressed against him, skin to skin, but she's also exhausted. She just wants the afternoon to be over with. So she doesn't fight him as he takes her arm and wraps it around his waist, or when he lays her hand on the shovel resting on his thigh. "Hold it there." He does the same with her other hand on the other side. "Hold this one here."

They ride along and soon she gives up altogether on personal space and lays her cheek on his back. He startles. "I'm sorry. I'm so tired," she mumbles.

"It's fine," he says, and hopes the rest of him can calm down.

They finally get to the house. Mason pries her hand off the shovel and drops it to the ground. He hops off before he comes around the other side for Maddie who is as limp as a wet noodle. She practically slides off Timber and lands right up against Mason, who feels so nice and sturdy. She feels like the leaning tower of Pisa.

He chuckles and pushes her upright. "Why don't we go grab something to eat? That should help you get your second wind."

She can't do anything but nod her head. "Sure. Let's do that."

She follows him to his truck and hauls herself up in his cab. She leans on the door for support on the way to town. "What do you feel like?" he asks.

She gives him a tired glance. "Drive through."

He nods his head. "Got it." He pulls up to the local café and hops out.

"Mason. Put on your shirt," she calls out after him. He

waves her off and keeps walking. She Snaps a pic of his back and sends it to Alex. Mason's going to give those old ladies something to talk about. She spies Lettie, the town gossip, making her way across the parking lot. Maddie ducks down sideways in the truck to lay on the seat and waits for a reply from Alex. She closes her eyes for a few minutes.

"Maddie?"

Maddie opens an eye and peeks up at him. Mason's at the driver's side window. "Yep."

"What're you doin'?"

"Tryin' to slow down the gossip train."

He grins. "It's a little too late for that. I already told the girl I'd be right back with your order."

"Why would you do that? You know what I like. We used to eat here every Saturday for like three years."

His face looks puzzled. He puts a key in his ear and itches like he does when he's nervous. "I don't know. Sometimes people's tastes change." He's so adorable, she thinks right before she decides she's losing her mind as thoughts of Mason and all his cuteness hit her upside the head.

"Alright, well. Just get me what I used to get," she answers absent-mindedly.

He grins. "Chicken fingers, extra fries, and a strawberry pop. Got it."

Barf. "No. I don't want that. I want chicken fingers, a salad with ranch, a side of tots, and a homemade lemonade or what-ever's closest to it."

"Alright. I'll try to remember all that." He gets an ornery look on his face. "You could go in with me and order it yourself."

She shakes her head. She can already hear the tongues wagging. "Nope, not doin' that."

He takes off at a jog. She falls back over on his side of the seat. She tries to slow down her thoughts, but she can't. Just like she can't help but notice that spending time with Mason is so easy. She can totally be herself, and he's okay with that.

She knows it wasn't anyone else's fault, but when she was at college, she always felt like she was trying to impress people because she was from a small town. She was always trying to show everyone she wasn't small town, that she could be a big city girl too. But sitting here now she can't fight the feeling that this place is also her home. She stares up at the truck ceiling. "Will I ever know where I fit in?" she wonders aloud.

She reaches her hand up to trace hearts on his truck ceiling. She takes a deep breath in. She smells him everywhere inside his truck. It stirs up emotions deep inside her she didn't know were there. Like a beautiful waterfall that hides around the next corner waiting to be discovered on a long hike through the woods.

Her head hurts. "This is crazy. I can't be falling for Mason French. He's my childhood friend. He's the boy who would run from me when I chased him with snakes, toads, and June bugs. He's the only boy I ever went skinny dipping with. Okay, we were five and he was in the water for less than five seconds because he was terrified of leeches, but still, it counts," she self-whispers. She feels even more crazy. She's thankful no one is there to hear her.

She runs a finger over the ridges of his steering wheel. "I can't be falling for him. I'm only in town for the summer, and then I'm leaving to go back to the city where I belong to fulfill my dream of leaving my thumbprint on the world through my writing. How can I write about places I've seen, things I've done, and emotions I've felt if I stay here? It's what I want, isn't it?" She sits up a little and peeks over the steering wheel just in time to see him whistling to himself as he walks toward the truck. *He's so hot.* Maddie decides she needs space between them so she can think.

Fourteen

Mason catches Maddie's eyes that peek over the steering wheel but pretends that he doesn't. Half the time he has no clue what goes on inside that girl's head, but he knows one thing for certain, if she were his girlfriend he wouldn't be bored. He almost trips over nothing in the parking lot at the idea that she would ever be his. He knows something's going on between them, but he also knows Maddie. She'll fight him to the bitter end. She's a never-say-die kind of girl. He can't help but grin despite his pain. She's the same old Maddie. She gives him a headache and-a-half, ties his stomach in knots, and makes him want things he can't have. Some habits are hard to break.

He looks toward the truck again. They're not dating and they're not together, but the attraction is definitely there. There's no denying that.

He fights feeling discouraged as he tries to think of reasons for her resistance. Is she really staying away because of the dumb feud between their families that's as old as Moses? Surely, she's outgrown that grudge. He frowns a little at the realization that she's so hard-headed if she really wanted to be with him, she would, and that's the kicker. He doesn't know if she does.

His head spins as he opens the truck door to find her lying upside down. Their eyes meet and that's when he sees it. She's holding on to something and she's not ready to let go. He's pretty sure it's not a guy, which is almost worse because he's pretty sure he could compete with another guy especially the one who just cheated on her. But if it's an idea she's got in her head he hasn't got a prayer. If there's one thing Mason knows, if you keep someone from dreaming, no matter how big or how small, you'll never feel like a winner.

He hops in the truck and hands over her food. "Here you go. I hope I got it right."

She flips open the container like she's starving. She pulls apart her chicken and waves her hands over it to cool it down just like when they were kids. "Dang, that chicken's hot," Maddie's Southern twang just popped out and boy if it doesn't ping off Mason's insides like shotgun scatter.

He busts out laughing and side-eyes her, so he won't lean over and kiss her. "Shoot, Maddie. It's ain't that hot."

She turns to look at him. "I've got sensitive lips. You don't know."

He gives her lips a good long look before he winks at her. "I know all about your lips, Maddie Dill. They're flawless."

She sobers up and blushes so hard. She stares him down. Emotions run freely over her face. She was never meant to be a poker player, at least not a very good one. First, she's hot, then she's fired up mad, and then she's all quiet. She elbows him so hard he almost drops his burger. "Hey! What was that for?"

She grins at him. "You're teasin' me. Can't I tease you?"

He frowns at her. "I s'pose, but your kind of teasin' leaves bruises." *Inside and out.*

She giggles and takes a bite of her chicken. She closes her eyes and lays her head back on the seat. "Man, what is it about this chicken? It's so good. I swear no one comes close to makin' chicken like Rosa's Café."

His nose is a little bent. He's feeling frustrated over her groaning over chicken. "Maybe it's not the restaurant. Maybe you just miss bein' home."

Her brown eyes fly open and she side-eyes him. "Nope. I think it's the cook. If it's one thing us southerners know how to do, it's fry chicken." She winks at him. "Or my rooster don't crow at dawn."

He snorts. "What does your rooster have to do with anything?"

She laughs and points two fingers holding chicken in the air. "Egg-zactly."

He shakes his head. "Darlin', you're a whole lotta hot air."

She stares out the window and pops a tater tot. "I'm a whole lotta somethin'," she mutters, but he can't tell if it's happy or sad. She turns back to him. "You ever wonder where you're supposed to be?"

He slurps his Coke. "Sittin' right here feels pretty good."

She rolls her eyes. "I'm serious."

He stares back at her. "So am I." She ducks her head and takes another bite of chicken. They eat in silence for a while. "Maybeweshouldn'ttakethatheiferoutthere." Her words all run together, and it takes a few seconds to register what she said.

He about chokes on his mouth full of fries. He gets them halfway down and turns the other way to look out his window. "What are you saying? We spent most of the day diggin' that hole. Of course we're takin' the heifer out there."

"I don't know. I mean, I could always go back and fill it back up. It'd be a lot easier than it was to dig up, that's for sure," she hem-haws around.

He shakes his head again. "Huh uh, Maddie. No way. We're takin' that heifer out there, and it's going to be tonight." His grey-eyed gaze burns into her brown eyes that show doubt. He can't believe this is happening. "Are you losing your nerve? I never thought I'd see the day," he goads her.

"Well, we could sleep on it. That's all I'm sayin'."

He shakes his head back and forth. "That's a terrible idea. I know if I wait even a day or two, you won't do it at all. I'm not putting all this effort into foolishness and then not doing it. This was all your idea anyway. It's high time somebody does something about this stupid feud between our families." He gives her a smirk. "Besides, aren't you the one who's all for democracy and coming together? Isn't it better to unite than divide?" He lays it on thick, but he doesn't care. He can't believe her trying to back out on him.

She sits back in her seat and crosses her arms on her chest. "Shut up, Mason. You're just tryin' to get to me with all your political talk. You don't care a whit what I believe or think."

He slaps the truck seat between them. "I do too." He glares at her. "Don't be tellin' me how I feel about you, Maddie. Don't even start."

"You just want this feud over because you want us." She stops. "I mean you want me."

Damn right I want you, Mason thinks as his jaw tightens.

She shuts up and looks out the window, away from Mason.

He reaches out and touches her arm, just barely. "What? What do I want between us?"

She swats at his hand. "Oh, stuff it, Mason. Either be a man and say what you want, or don't, but don't try to make me say it just because you're a coward."

His whole face heats up as thoughts whirl around in his mind. He's not a coward. He just can't stand rejection, especially not from Maddie Dill. "I know what I want. I've known what I wanted since we were sixteen-years-old and probably even before that. I was just too ignorant and afraid to recognize it."

She whips her head around and stares him down like she's daring him to say it just so she can burn his words like ashes between them. "What, Mason? What do you want?" She spits the words out. He watches her carefully and doesn't say another word. She hates silence more than anything else. *I want you to want me, Maddie, that is all I want*, runs through his mind like a broken record. But why can't he just say it? Instead, he sits there like an idiot staring all hangdog at the only girl he's ever really loved. But it doesn't matter because she doesn't love him back.

He breaks their awkwardly long gaze with a big old cowboy grin he totally doesn't feel. "Let's go get that heifer and toss her down a hole." He puts his truck in reverse and floors it, throwing up gravel. "That's what I want."

She props her bare feet up on the dash. She wiggles her toes. "If that's what you want to do."

He nods his head like he's five all over again. "More than anything in the world," he speaks all in earnest.

She giggles. "French Fry, you're a weird-o."

He bops his head back and forth before glancing over at her. "But I'm your weird-o."

MYSTERY COUPLE

LOVE HAS ITS OWN
TIME AND SPACE

After college I was done being a small-town girl. My goal was to see the world and advance in my career and I happily did both. I landed in a big city where I met lots of great guys, but they weren't really my type. We went out and had a lot of fun. It was perfect for me as a quiet, introverted girl to surround myself with men searching for their prince charming. One of my many friends wanted to see me happy too, and he kept telling me to join Match.com, something outside my comfort zone.

But then on a late November night I got up the nerve and put myself out there. A few weeks later I got a wink. We chatted back and forth. He seemed like a great guy, but we lived too far apart. I went on a few dates with other guys who lived closer but there was something about the one guy.

Then came the day I was staying near his hometown for the weekend, before flying out to see some of my family. We agreed to meet at a restaurant. When I saw him across the lot, I just felt like he was The One. The next week I showed his profile to my best friend, and she told her mom to come look at my future husband. He showed my profile to his mom and she said to her husband, "come look at my future daughter-in-law."

We've been together eighteen years and married for thirteen. In my younger days I never would have imagined myself, a small-town Kansas girl marrying a man from Laos, a country halfway around the world. But we met and fell in love, and I wouldn't trade my life for anything.

- Maddie Dill
The Daily Chase

Fifteen

Maddie doesn't know whether to laugh or cry when she recalls just a few months ago she was applying for internships and menial journalism jobs all across the United States. And now here she is sitting around with Mason, hanging out behind the big tree in the middle of the field like an idiot waiting for two old men to show up to save the sacrificial lamb, or in this case a baby heifer happily chewing on grass and hay at the bottom of a man-made hole. She glances at the tree line once more and hopes they hid that ATV good enough. Just about the time she thinks no one's coming, she hears a motor running followed by lots of shouting.

"It's over there." Maddie instinctively sinks to her butt at the sound of her grandpa Dean's voice. She doesn't want to be seen. Mason remains standing as he looks down at her with a smirk.

"What if they see you?" she whisper shouts.

He raises one eyebrow. "Those two are about as blind as bats with tunnel vision. They ain't gonna see me. The only thing they're looking for is livestock."

She peeks out from behind Mason's knee because she's squatting. Sure enough, the four-wheeler pulls up to the hole. His grandpa Steve hops off first. "How'd that hole get there?"

Steve stares hard at her grandpa who crawls off the four-wheeler. Then he throws his hands in the air. "Heck if I know,

Steve. Are you sayin' I dug that hole and drug your sorry ass out here to admire my handiwork?"

Steve shrugs. "I wouldn't put it past ya."

"I'm way past the days of pulling tricks on you, old man," Grandpa says, shaking his head. "Too much excitement sets my pacemaker off."

Steve smirks. "Well, then. I guess your wife finally got lucky." Grandpa shoves Steve so hard he almost trips. Maddie holds in a gasp. "Watch it, Dean. You about shoved me down that hole."

"You shut up about my wife," Maddie's grandpa roars.

"Alright, alright," Steve says, throwing up his hands. "It was just a joke. Calm down." The two old men stare down the hole. Steve scratches his head. "Don't you think it's a little funny there's a rope and a stake in the ground close by? I feel like someone set us up."

Grandpa taps his foot. "I don't know, Steve. It could've been anyone playing this trick, but we still gotta get that heifer out. It shouldn't be down there so long. It might get thirsty."

Steve sighs. "I guess, but I've half a mind to call that ornery grandson of mine. Something tells me French Fry and Dill Pickle are up to their shenanigans again." He whips out his phone.

Maddie squeezes Mason's knee hard. He looks down at her. "Silence your phone," she mouths.

His face is full of question. She reaches up and grabs his phone from his back pocket to turn the volume off. He grins ear-to-ear. "You touched my butt."

Her face flames. "Grow up, Mason," she whispers as she messes with his settings.

A phone goes off like a siren. She peeks out at them again. Her grandpa's fumbling with his phone in his shirt pocket. He finally opens it and gets it to his ear. "Yeah. Uh-huh. Yeah. Alright. We'll be there. What? I'm with Steve. Of course, it's business."

Dean shuts his flip phone. Steve stares at him. "Was your wife chewing your ass again for hanging out with me?"

Grandpa looks embarrassed. "Maybe."

Steve shakes his head. "Well. I guess we'd better not tell her about our weekly poker game that's been going on for the past ten years or so."

Maddie's mind is blown. *What?* She can hardly believe her grandpa's been having poker night with his mortal enemy. She wonders if Mason knows. She looks up to see his head hanging in his hands. She would guess that he knows.

Her grandpa coughs. "I don't know what the big deal is. My friends have been dying off for the past five years anyways, and this town is only so big. I don't think Pearl wants me to drive twenty miles just to make new friends."

Steve claps a hand on his shoulder. "Relax. One thing at time. What was that phone call about?"

Dean claps a hand to his head. "Oh, crap. My prized Delilah that was impregnated with your bull, Samson, is having a heck of a time." Dean stomps his foot and points his arthritic finger at Steve once more. "I told you your bull was too big, but you were so starry-eyed over the end product you couldn't see what that labor would do to my Delilah. You'd better pray it doesn't kill her or you owe me some money."

Steve laughs. "Ha. Whatever you say, Dean. If you didn't want my prize bull sniffing around your cow, maybe you shouldn't have named her Delilah." Maddie holds in her giggle at his biblical joke. Steve crosses his arms on his chest. "Besides, my Samson's worth at least ten of your Delilah's, so dry up about it. She's going to be fine. I know a trick or two about getting out of slippery situations."

Grandpa Dean snorts. "I just bet you do."

Steve hops on. "Come on, old man. We ain't got time to waste. We've got to save Delilah." Grandpa Dean climbs on the back of the ATV, and off they go.

Sixteen

Mason looks down at Maddie. He can see she's madder than a wet hornet. "That's just great. How are we going to get back to the farm now," she yells up at him.

He raises his eyebrows. "Why are we going to the farm? They'll take care of it."

She slaps his leg. "If Delilah's in trouble, they're going to need help."

"How we going to explain that we know about Delilah?" He frowns down at her.

She rolls her eyes. "Those two old men drop in on whoever and whenever they please. I don't know why I can't do the same."

He sighs. "Let's just use the ATV then."

She makes another face. "Mason. We can't do that. Then they'll know we were out here."

He can't believe how ridiculous she's being. "Are you saying we're walking to the farm from here?"

"I don't know." She bites her lip. "All I'm saying is we can't trail them on the ATV. Then they'll know what we've been up to."

"You're exhausting. I've already spent myself digging a

gosh-darn hole. I don't really feel like running a few miles just to hide an ATV."

She grimaces. "Who said anything about running. I can speed walk it."

He looks back all cocky like, hoping maybe the idea of jogging across the fields will knock some sense into her and her stupid stubborn ways. She crosses her arms on her chest. Her stubborn face digs in. He sighs. "Running it is then."

She pouts just a little. "I should've brought my horse."

He snorts and shakes his head. "Yeah, that totally would've given us away. Your horse doesn't know how to hide."

She grins at him. "Yeah, you're probably right about that."

He can't help but chuckle. "Excuse me, did you just tell me I was right?"

She rolls her eyes. "Come on, country boy, it's time to cut across the pastures." She takes off jogging and calls out behind her. "Better hope you don't find any snakes."

He looks down at his boots. "Why did I wear boots?" He starts off at a jog behind her. She's way up there. He can't believe he forgot she can really run. He tries to set a pace for himself but it's pathetic. He may be built for digging but he sure ain't built for running. He jogs as far as he can before he stops to walk. He can't help but laugh at himself as he strides across the dark field, watching the full moon light up blades of grass. "Maddie Dill. Following you around is all kinds of tiresome, but I can't seem to stop," he whispers into the still night air. He looks ahead between his huffing and puffing. She's over the hill and gone. "Go on, Maddie. Don't worry about me," he calls out. "Just do what you always do," he mutters.

She doesn't answer. He keeps on at his walk/jog pace until he reaches the barn a good forty minutes later. If anyone notices him walking in, no one says anything. His eyebrows raise at the sight. Maddie's in there with the two grandpas. Delilah's mooing up a storm. A hoof sticks out her back end. He holds down his barf. Labor slime is so disgusting. Delilah stomps her feet and thrashes her head around. Maddie's up by her neck, patting her and crooning. So far as Mason can tell, it doesn't seem to be helping.

Mason's Grandpa Steve clears his throat. "Anyone got a guitar?"

Dean snorts. "What the hell you want a guitar for? You gonna sing us to sleep?"

Steve stomps his foot. "I'm going to sing to Delilah. It'll help her relax. You'll see."

Mason thinks Grandpa Steve's full of crap but he has no suggestions, so why not? He turns and follows Maddie out the barn door. They run into the house. She steps into a side room and brings out a banjo. "That's not exactly a guitar, Maddie."

She slams it into his chest. "It's got strings and it's the closest thing we've got, Mason. Adapt."

They hurry back out to the barn. Steve snatches the banjo from Mason. He starts strumming and singing some song about cheating Clarita and her band of banditas. Mason snickers in surprise. He didn't know Steve had that kind of humor in him. He glances at Delilah. She's stopped her thrashing and kicking. Maddie yanks on a pair of rubber kitchen gloves. "I'm going in," she announces.

Mason wants to run for the door. Is Maddie going to do what he thinks she's going to do? The next thing he knows, her hand disappears up to her shoulder in Delilah—somewhere he doesn't want to see. Maddie turns to smile over at Dean while Mason's skin crawls. "She's relaxing."

More of the cow slips out. Mason waits for Maddie to jump back, but she stands her ground. She holds onto the half of the calf that hangs out. Mason vows not to hurl. "Come on, girl. It's okay. You can do it," Maddie croons in between Steve's questionable lyrics as he strums away on his banjo. What's going on with Dean? His face gets redder by the second as he stares at Steve. This is the weirdest Monday night Mason's ever had. He watches in horror as the calf slips all the way out and Maddie goes to the floor. She's covered with blood and slime. Mason leans over and puts his head near his weak knees before he embarrasses himself. He's thoroughly traumatized as he sinks down the far wall.

He sneaks reluctant glances at Maddie who lays beneath the calf. Her grandpa swipes a few fingers in its mouth and drags out what looks like mucus or saliva by the gallon. *Barf.* Maddie looks over at Mason with her big brown eyes. Her red hair spreads out on the barn floor. Her freckles are hidden beneath some kind of afterbirth. She grins from ear to ear. "Isn't she beautiful?" she asks as her head literally peeks out from beneath the calf's back end. Maddie is clearly delusional. There's nothing beautiful about any of this.

"She's something," Mason chokes out.

Dean turns on Steve who strums his banjo. "It figures you would sing a song about cheating."

Steve stops playing his banjo. He waves his hand in Delilah's direction. "It's her favorite song. That's not my fault."

"She's a cow. She doesn't have a favorite song. You just played that song to make me mad!"

Steve guffaws. "Make you mad. Mad about what? I just saved your cow from dying."

Dean crosses his arms on his chest. "Whatever, Steve. Maybe I'm talking about your family stealing the woman on the ship, or the time your family stole my super-secret family recipe." He stomps his foot for good measure. "Who knows what else your family stole from me!"

Mason's grandpa shakes his head. "The only thing I might've stolen from you, Dean, is your good sense." Mason chokes down laughter. Maddie's eyes meet Mason's. She's not laughing. Mason studies her some more while Dean's face gets redder and redder. Mason hopes he doesn't pass out on the floor.

Mason rethinks their conversation about cheating. What the heck are they talking about? Maddie looks as surprised as him, so he doesn't think she knows anything. Steve snorts. "No one knows whose recipe that was, Dean. All I know is my family made the best fried pickles this county's ever tasted, and it's not my fault if my family restaurant made a bunch of money off them. If your family had the recipe first, what difference does it make? They were too afraid to try to patent them. That's not my fault."

Dean stomps his foot. "You don't know that. And just because my family didn't want to profit off a family recipe doesn't give your family the right to steal it, patent it, and call it their own."

Maddie's eyes narrow at Mason. "Fried pickles." She points an accusing finger at Steve. "You *stole* the recipe for the fried pickles?"

Mason's grandpa shrugs. "Hey. It was the eighties. Everyone was lookin' to make a quick buck." He stares at Dean. "Not everyone had a bunch of land laying around as a fallback."

Dean's face turns bright red. "I'm not going to apologize for being born fortunate."

Steve snorts. "Well, I'm not going to apologize for lacking, or seizing an opportunity." He stands up and walks out toward the barn door with the banjo. Mason follows along behind him.

"Hey," Dean yells. "Leave my banjo, or are you going to steal that too?"

Steve lays the banjo down with exaggerated care. He turns back to face Dean. "I don't want your fallin-apart banjo. It ain't worth much without my gifted hands, anyway." He walks out the door all slumped, then climbs onto the ATV. Steve turns to Mason. "Climb on, French Fry. Don't worry. I've got headlights."

Mason coughs. "Man, Maddie sure got mad in a hurry."

Steve laughs. "Yeah. That apple don't fall far from the tree."

Mason shakes his head and thinks even though grandpa might be right, he doesn't have to like it.

Seventeen

Maddie and her grandpa stay in the barn and clean up the calf. He glances at his watch. "Mercy sakes. I didn't realize how late it was. We'd better head inside." He looks over at her. "You gonna name your calf?"

She claps her hands with excitement. "Yes. I haven't done this in years," she says with no small amount of embarrassment. Once again, she feels torn between feeling like she's left everyone behind. Even though she knows her family is proud of her and all of her big dreams, she knows they wish she didn't have such a strong desire to move so far away. She leans on the wall and watches the newborn calf as her mom cleans her up. Maddie feels lost. She thinks of the argument she heard earlier between Steve and Dean, and it hits her. "I'm naming her 'Eighties Baby'."

Dean looks at her like she's nuts. "What kind of name is that? Don't you think something like Thistle or Rose would be better?"

Maddie giggles. "Nope. 'Eighties Baby' is it. That's her name." She glances at her grandpa to see if he's thinking about the argument he just had with Steve. She can't really tell.

Her grandpa shakes his head back and forth before patting her on the head. "I guess you really are a journalist. You've sure got a way with words. Wait'll your grandma hears about this name."

She follows along behind her grandpa, but not before hanging back to steal one more glance at the adorable Eighties Baby. Maddie recalls the look on Mason's face. He looked like he was about to lose his lunch. She can't believe he hasn't outgrown his squeamishness even though it is kind of cute. And that's when she remembers the heifer down the hole. "Oh, crap balls."

"What did you say?" her grandpa mumbles from up ahead.

"Nothing, Grandpa. I'm just talkin' to myself," she answers.

Maddie whips out her phone and texts Mason.

Maddie: Up for a midnight caper? Alex's calf is still in the hole.

She jams her phone back in her jeans pocket and walks up to grandpa's house. She clears her throat. "Did Steve really steal the family recipe," Maddie takes a deep breath, "or did he win it in a poker game?" The second half of her question flies out like an afterthought. By the look on her grandpa's face, she'd bet money he heard it, just like she'd bet money they've been playing cards for way longer than ten years. Her grandpa sits down on the front step. She plops down beside him.

He pats her knee. "Maddie. Sometimes it's easier to go along with what your wife thinks is best instead of to argue with her." The desperation in his voice shakes her to the core. "It was a pride thing. I couldn't not go to poker night just because she said no." Her grandpa scratches his neck. "Anyways, I think she knew. Wives always know."

Maddie shakes her head. "If you lost the recipe in a poker game and let Grandma think they stole it, that's pretty crappy, Grandpa."

Grandpa throws up his hands. "What was I supposed to do? Own up to losing the family recipe in a game of cards and forfeit my seat at the poker table by taking it back? I couldn't do that. It was much easier to let her think they stole it. In a way, they kind of did. Steve didn't have to call my bluff. He could have turned in his hand." Dean's voice gets all quiet with his last sentence.

"You're just sore 'cause he was a better poker player than you." Maddie can't believe she's defending Mason's family.

She waits for his anger. She's surprised when her grandpa laughs. "Probably so." He bumps into her. "We're the same, little girl. I can't hide my emotions any better than you can, so don't go playing any poker." He gives her a wink. "At least not with Mason French."

She draws her arms around her knees and rests her chin there. "Your generation was a funny thing, Grandpa."

He chuckles. "I suppose so, but I guess I'd rather keep some things under wraps instead of have it all over the internet for everyone to see." He nudges her again. "My generation may have been close-mouthed, but we sure had a lot of fun." He looks up at the sky. "I worry about the day kids lose the wonder of the cold dew on the fresh morning grass between their toes, or a ray of sunshine sneaking through the window to warm them, or the thrill of sleeping all night in a car down a country backroad and waking up to nothing but the sounds of nature." He shakes his head. "Bein' raised a country boy ain't all that bad. We love the simple things."

She sighs. "When you put it that way, Grandpa, it all sounds pretty nice." She shoulder bumps him. "I think you were born to be a poet."

Her grandpa smiles. "My grandfather was kind of a poet. I don't know that he wrote any poetry, but he loved to recite it." He stares up at the sky. "He was a minister too. He taught me what it means to love Jesus and to love God. He taught me what it means to see a Creator in most anything, but you have to look for Him to see Him." He stares up in the night sky. "I've been to the city, and it's alright, but nothing beats a night in a wide-open field under a canopy of stars. It's just me and nature out here, the way God intended man and Earth to be. That's the way I like it."

She sits for a while and thinks about his words as she stares up at the sky. "It sure is peaceful out here."

"Mmm hmmm. It settles the soul."

She leans on his shoulder. "You're definitely a poet."

He snorts. "I wrote a line or two along the way." He looks over at me with an ornery grin. "How do you think I got your grandmother?"

She sneaks a peek at him. "That's pretty romantic, Grandpa." A lightbulb goes off. "Hey, can I write an article about you and grandma for the paper?"

Her grandpa pulls a face. "Haven't you been listening to me? I don't *need* my love for your grandma written down to know it happened." He pats his chest. "I have it all right here."

Her eyes well up. "I'm sorry. I just thought it'd be nice for my generation to read about what a good old-fashioned love story is."

He stares her down. "Go sell your pitch on someone else's doorstep, Maddie. Your request has merit, but you forget where your stubbornness came from. I'm not budging."

The backdoor flies open. Grandma Pearl scowls down at the two of them. "Landsakes alive. You two gonna sit out here long enough to get eaten up by mosquitoes?" She nudges Grandpa with her foot. "Come on, old man, I'm getting tired. Let's go to bed."

Grandpa hops up with a quickness Maddie didn't know he possessed. "Yes, ma'am. You don't have to tell me twice." Maddie grins and thinks to herself, *stubborn my butt, Grandpa. You jump when she says jump.*

She looks up at her Grandma Pearl who lingers on the step. "I'm just going to sit out here a while longer and enjoy the stars. They sure are pretty tonight."

Grandma harrumphs. "Suit yourself." The door shuts. Maddie rests her chin on her knees as she hears more grumbling and mumbling behind it.

Maddie glances down at her phone sitting on the step beside her. "Mason had better answer pretty soon. That calf shouldn't stay down there overnight, but I don't want to rescue it by myself either," Maddie mutters just as vibration goes off near her butt.

MASON:

Meet me at the end of your drive in ten.

Miniature fireworks go off inside her though she tries to ignore them.

MADDIE:

10-4. Operation rescue heifer is underway.

MASON:

Maddie, why can't you talk normal?

Maddie laughs as she reads his text. She hits him back.

MADDIE:

I'm a journalist, Mason. This is my normal.

Maddie opens the back door quietly and locks her grandma's backdoor from the inside, a sure sign she won't be back tonight. She runs to the barn to dunk her head under the hose and give it a good scrubbing. The water is freezing but it's better than labor slime in her hair and on her face. She whips her wet hair up into a makeshift bun and starts the long walk down her driveway. Even though she's pretty sure her grandpa lost that family recipe in a poker game fair and square, she's still annoyed with Mason's family for taking it. They could have given it back or at least not paraded it all over town like it was theirs.

And even though Maddie knows that's not Mason's fault either, Maddie is agitated. She stalks down the driveway and racks her brain to try to think of a way to prove to the town that the recipe was her family's first. She figures if she can do that, her grandpa won't be so mad at his grandpa. But more importantly, at least she could recover a little family pride being her grandpa is the reason they lost their recipe in the first place. "Darn men and their darn bettin' and gamblin' just to pass the time. Why can't they do something more productive like crocheting or baking pies," she grumbles into the darkness.

She stands around at the end of her grandpa's driveway and tries not to flinch when she hears the coyotes' howls. She tells herself they carry on the wind and they're not just across the road even though they sound it. Just about the time she's ready to chicken out and make Mason drive all the way up the drive, she spies a pair of headlights coming up the road. She breathes a sigh of relief as he comes to a stop.

"Sheesh. I thought I'd never get my grandpa off this thing. He wanted to go out there to get the calf with me. In the middle of the night, in the dark. He could've fallen down the hole," Mason grumbles. He grins at her. "I think he knows we're going out there and he wanted to see how worried he could get me by making me think I'd be stuck with him instead of you."

She lays a tired hand on her hip. "You gonna keep yakkin' or you gonna take me out to rescue the calf that's probably scared to death by now?"

He opens his mouth to answer but shuts it again. She puts a hand on his shoulder and climbs on the ATV behind him. "Hold on. It might get a little bumpy," his voice growls at her as she leans into him.

She tries to ignore the fact that being this close to Mason makes her feel bumpy on the inside. He hits the gas, and they start down the road. Before too long, he starts off across the field. They drive through the grass and over the little hill. The tall grass tickles their ankles. She breathes in deep, knowing it'll be a long time before she forgets the smell of Mason mixed with the smell of nature and the cool night air kissing her cheeks as they ride along beneath the night sky. She can't think of a more perfect way to spend a night. Her thoughts sober her right up and she can't help but wonder if maybe she really is just a small-town girl like Alex wishes. Or is it just grandpa's romantic stargazing words whispering in her ears?

Eighteen

They head down the hill and Mason slows way down praying they find their way to that hole in the dark before they flip the ATV on the bumps. They motor along as quietly as possible. Just when he thinks he's out of luck, he hears a mooing. He almost slams right into the pole from the side. He swerves and comes to a stop just in time. She flies off the back and lands on her butt in the shallow end of the creek bed. She comes out of the water whooping, hollering, and shivering to beat the band. "Ice water in my pants. Ooh, that's freezing." He laughs out loud, even though there's murder in her eyes. "Mason French. It's not funny!"

He can't help it. He laughs harder. It's a whole lot of funny. "You should see your face. Ooh, boy. You're freezing your arse."

Her eyes light up. She always did love the word 'arse', though he doesn't know why. She gives him a shove. "Let's get that whiner out of there before she has the coyotes circling."

He grabs a hold of the rope tied to the pole and gives it a good tug. It doesn't budge. "I'm going down. Hold that light for me, would ya?"

She holds up her cell phone and he starts down. He hates to admit it's a lot creepier going down in the hole in the dark. It isn't long and he's at the bottom.

"How you doing?" she asks.

"Fine. Hold your horses. All I have to do now is the hard part. You know, the part where I haul the calf over my shoulders, balance her there, and climb out." He grunts and groans as he hauls her up in place and prays she lays still. He starts back up the rope. Every muscle in his body burns. He tells himself he did this a few hours ago so he can do it again now. But it's been a long day and going down was a heck of a lot easier than going up. He continues to grunt and groan with his efforts.

"Mason, are you alright?"

No, I'm hauling a 200-pound calf up a rope attached to a stake in the ground and I hope it holds all of us. "Yeah," he manages. Barely.

His arms burn like fire. He doesn't know if he can do this, but he can't stop either. If he stops, he'll never get going again. He tugs and pulls with all his might. By some miracle, he reaches the top. Maddie helps get the calf off him as he leans over the edge with her. He somehow manages to pull himself completely out of the hole. Mason lays down flat on the ground with his arms out to both sides. The calf starts to walk toward him. He throws an arm in front of it. "Maddie, get her away from the hole. I ain't goin' down there again," he hollers.

Maddie scrambles to lead the calf a good distance away. He stares up at the sky and tries to breathe normally but it's a long time coming. "I'm so tired I could just lay here and never get up," he moans as he closes his eyes. Minutes fly by. He's almost asleep from physical exhaustion, even though his knees on down dangle over the edge of the hole. He sighs. "For once the grass feels good on the back of my neck." He waits for a response from Maddie, who's strangely quiet and out of sight. He's too tired to turn his head. He spies fireflies in the distance. He watches as they grow closer. They dance over the creek bed in the light of the moon as they flicker along. A small breeze comes off the creek. A few fireflies float toward him. He smiles to himself as he rolls over to look for Maddie who stands off to the side, holding loosely to the rope around the heifer's neck as they hover in the grass. "It's another firefly moon night tonight," he all but whispers.

"What do you mean?" Maddie's words are all softness and

light, just like the unexplainable moment of peace that settles over the both of them.

He blinks. "Remember all those summer nights we spent with the fireflies?"

She laughs. "Yeah, fireflies are the only bug that doesn't make you squirm like a girl."

He frowns just a little as he thinks to himself, *leave it to Maddie to try to ruin our good times together*. "Whatever. Just never mind."

She turns away from him. "Can you believe we're adults now?" She sounds so serious.

He coughs. "Yeah, I guess."

She turns back to look at him again. "What does that mean, exactly?"

He recalls the many conversations at his dinner table growing up. "It means a thirty-year house loan, taking trips we can't afford, driving cars we can't afford, having children we can't afford, and lovin' every minute of it."

She grins down at him. "Well. Here's to our last summer of freedom."

He smiles up at her from the ground. "Yep. To freedom." A look passes between them. In that moment, Mason knows without a doubt that his heart belongs to Maddie Dill. It always has. And one day, come hell or high water, her heart will belong to him.

MYSTERY COUPLE

SISTERS KNOW BEST

My future husband and I went to the same junior high and high school. We knew who each other was but that was about it. My husband's sister had been in my mom's English class in high school. They must have been talking about girls at home because she showed him my picture in the yearbook and told him he should ask me out.

Not long after that conversation he and I were asked to be servers together at the junior/senior prom. I got tired of waiting for him to call me about it and so I called him and asked him to be a server with me. When I called him up to ask him out, he told me he was going to call me to ask me to the same event.

The prom was still a month away, so he asked me to go watch the high school play with him – it was *"Paint Your Wagon"* that year. We had a wonderful time and continued dating through the rest of high school.

When we graduated, we separated to go to different colleges. But after one semester I transferred to the college he attended, and I loved it there. It felt like we started up right where we left off. We laughed, walked, talked, and studied together. We got married in our junior year of college and have enjoyed each other's company ever since. We've been married for forty-eight years.

- Maddie Dill
The Daily Chase

Nineteen

Something in Mason's eyes shakes Maddie from her head to her toes. It's a feeling so strong she looks down at the ground, half expecting the Earth to move beneath her feet. *What just happened, and why does Mason look all sure of himself?* she wonders before she turns around to go stand a little closer to the lost heifer.

She stands beside the happy heifer who mindlessly chews on some grass. Maddie stares up at the moon. "Well, at least we got to the bottom of a more recent family quarrel, but what're we gonna do about it?" she mutters and looks down at the mute calf. Maddie gives her a nudge in the side and swats at her butt. "You're no help." The heifer looks up with sad calf eyes. Maddie feels a little bad until she remembers she has to wrangle her heaviness all the way home. She wanders over toward Mason, dragging the heifer behind her. "I'm driving. You're carrying the heifer."

He groans from his position on the ground. "Fine."

She digs her fingernails into her palms and thinks of their grandpas fighting in the barn. It was so tiresome and sad. "There's got to be a simple solution to this ridiculousness. I know there is."

"What are you talking about now?" he asks as she stands over him.

"I'm talking about our family feud. We have to put a stop to it."

"Are you agreeing with me?" he asks. He looks amused.

She rolls her eyes. "Sure." Her stomach churns. "What if we had like a cook off?"

He blinks a few times, as if he doesn't comprehend what she is saying. "How do you mean?"

She pauses. "Well, you know how they have the half-Valentine dinner every summer? We could do it then because there will already be a crowd there, or whatever."

He frowns. "Just what are you proposing, Maddie Dill?"

She smiles as she warms to her idea. "What if you and I had a miniature contest there? You could make a batch of pickles and I could make a batch of pickles. Whoever wins the contest gets to claim the recipe as their own. And that would settle the matter once and for all between our families about who owns the pickle recipe."

"Hmm. I don't know. That's not entirely fair. Dill pickles are like your thing. I've never made them before." He smiles up at her. "I won't be the sole reason my family loses their good name after they worked so hard to stamp their name on something that became so well known."

Her temper flares just a little. "You're impossible." She stomps her foot. "You need to stop whining and try. You'll have all summer to perfect them."

He shakes his head back and forth. "No can do, not without an additional item." He raises his eyebrows at her. "How about we make it interesting? We both make pickles and seasoned French fries. Fries are more up my alley."

She coughs. "I've never made fries and you know this. It'll probably be a disaster."

"Just try. You have all summer to figure it out," he mimics her.

She stops her foot from kicking him in the head as he continues to lay there with the sexiest bedhead she's ever seen. "Fine. Now get up off the ground. I want to go home."

He grins up at her. "I'm so glad we agree. You'll see. Making both will make it more even. You've never made French fries and I've never made fried pickles. This way it's fair on both sides. And we both use the family recipe on both things and then the diners vote on it."

She nods her head. "Sounds like a plan, Stan." She hesitates. "But what if it's a tie?"

He laughs. "When have you ever known this town to be split down the middle, even?"

She rolls her eyes. "Plenty of times."

He slaps the ground. "I've got it. We can get a couple of food connoisseurs to come out and taste our goods. We can make it all legit and everything."

She giggles at the thought of a foodie tasting her mediocre cooking. "Are you for real?"

He sits up with some effort. "Yeah, like totes."

She cringes at his phrase. "What the heck did you just say?"

He looks a little embarrassed in the moonlight. "Totes?"

She snorts. "I hate that word. What are you like a VSCO boy now?"

He tips the front of his baseball hat over his face. "I'm not even gonna pretend to know what you be sayin' right now."

She steps over to him and lays a hand on his shoulder. "What I'm sayin' slacker, is that we need to get that calf back to its momma, and I need to get to bed. It's gonna be another early morning of going over sappy love stories." She sighs inside with contentment that she hopes she manages to keep out of her irritated tone.

"Love stories? What are you talking about?" His face is full of questions.

She blinks. "Didn't I tell you? I'm now interning at the paper and my first assignment is the half-Valentine local love stories. I write them and then people have to guess who they are."

He snorts. "Oh, yeah. I think I heard something about you reading through everybody's meet-cutes." He pokes her ankle hard. "Does that sting a little, having to read happily ever after stories?"

She glares down at him. "No, it doesn't, but thanks for your heartfelt concern." She looks off in the distance. "I'm surprised you know what meet-cute means. You been reading teenage books or something?" She grins as she shifts to teasing him once more.

He winks at her. "Hey, girl. I've been around more than you think."

She pinches the skin at the base of his neck. "Now that I can believe."

He shrugs and rubs the sore spot from her mean pinch. "I know the 4-1-1. I know the language they use on the streets. I'm hip with the next generation."

She laughs out loud. "The fact that you just used the word 'hip' tells me you are not totally in sync with the next generation, but that's alright. They make fun of my outdated journalistic language, but then they use words that wouldn't exist if not for the internet."

"You know, you sound like your mother just now."

"That may be, but our mommas knew a thing or two and I was raised to respect my parents."

His teasing face turns serious. "You're a girl after my own heart, Maddie Dill. You truly are."

There's so much emotion in his voice, she suffocates with it. She clears her throat. "All I know is that calf needs a ride home and I've got things to do in the morning. We need to go."

He crawls the rest of the way off the ground and stumbles toward the four-wheeler like a ninety-year-old man. "Dang, I'm sore all over. Tomorrow's going to be twice as bad."

She half-drags the calf over to the four-wheeler. He strains as he hauls the calf over his lap. Maddie climbs in front. She turns to Mason. "You need to get some Salonpas to help with your sore muscles. Just be sure and drink plenty of water. Those things will dehydrate you."

He leans in and rests his head on her shoulder. His hot breath falls on her ear. "Yes, ma'am."

Mason wakes up with sore arms and the stupid pickle-frying contest on the brain. He hops in his truck and drives down to Rosa's Café. He moseys inside and sits down at the front bar with a cup of coffee so he can eye the pastries behind the glass up close and personal. After a lot of thought, he decides to go with his favorites—strawberry crepes with whipped cream. Little, brown-eyed Rosa bustles out of her kitchen doors with a smile in her little white apron that has a big red rose in the middle. "Que pasa, mi nino? What can I do for you?"

"I'll take the strawberry crepes, please."

She scrawls his order on her little tablet. "Anything else?" she asks. Her quick brown eyes dart here and there, not missing a thing.

He leans in toward Rosa across the bar. "Say, Rosa. What do you think about teaching me a few things in the kitchen?"

Her eyes light up. She rests her chin on her palms to stare back at him like a little girl with stars in her eyes. "Like how to make fried pickles and French fries?"

He can't believe how easy this is. He slaps the counter. "Yeah, exactly like that."

Rosa slaps the counter right back. "No can do, French Fry. You're going to have to do this one on your own."

He stumbles over her rejection with one question, how did Rosa know what he was making, unless... "Has Maddie already been here?"

She gives him a wink. "She sure has. You just missed her."

He shakes his head and taps the counter. "Rosa. I can't believe you're going to teach Maddie how to cook, but not me."

She laughs again. "I'm not teaching either of you. You're adults now. You have college degrees and everything. You figure it out." She raises an eyebrow. "Maybe the two of you should cook together. They say good chemistry makes for delicious cooking."

He studies Rosa. "Really?"

Rosa giggles as she meanders down the counter to fill old Dennis's coffee cup. "No, but why the heck not? It makes sense to me," she continues in English with her heavy Spanish accent, betraying her native tongue. Mason loves how she rolls her "R's every time Rosa says, "my name is Rosa," even if he can't figure out how to do it.

He turns away from the sassy cook. "Maddie doesn't want to cook with me. That would require her being around me. She sure as heck doesn't want to be seen with me, at least not in public," he grumps.

Rosa rolls her eyes at his whining. "Don't you know anything, Romeo? That girl likes you. That's why she's running away. She's avoiding her feelings." Rosa sneaks out from behind her counter and gives his arm a squeeze. "What you've got to do is stick around. Stay close by. Hover. Torment her a little. Make sure she knows what she's missing out on."

He returns to the bar and studies Rosa from where he sits. "And here all this time I thought you'd been raised a nun."

Rosa throws back her head and laughs. "I most certainly am not a nun. I know how to have fun and cut loose, but I have clients who live here. They are worth every penny I earn, so I keep it pretty mild these days." She gives him another wink. "I was... how you say…a player back in my day. Trust me, I know the price of letting *the one* get away." Rosa moves on down the counter with her wash rag, scrubbing away.

He clears his throat. "Well. It sounds like you know a thing or two about love."

Rosa laughs again, but it sounds a little bitter. "Who said anything about love? I'm all about chasing the fish and catchin' the fish. Once I have one, I throw it back in again."

He stares at Rosa like she's crazy. "Why would you do that?"

She looks at him like he doesn't have a clue. "Do you think men are the only people who get bored in the relationship? Women do too. Everyday. We don't want an affair, but we want to feel the excitement of one, but we also want to feel noticed and cherished. We like to feel like we're the only girl in a man's universe. That's all."

He snorts. "Shoot, Rosa. You sure ask for a lot of a guy."

She sneaks up closer to him. "I've seen the way you look at Maddie. She's your whole world."

"I know that. I'm pretty sure Maddie knows too, but what if she doesn't want to be my whole world?"

Rosa pats his arm. "It'll be alright. You'll see." She winks at him again. "Just remember your name."

He's never felt so lost. "What does that mean?"

Rosa throws her hands in the air. "Mason stands for Mason jar."

He blinks. "Yeah, so?"

Rosa stares him down like he should be able to read her mind. "And what do you put in mason jars?"

He shrugs. "Candles?"

She smacks his arm. "Fireflies, ya nut!"

He thinks little Rosa's lost all her marbles. "Okay?"

She crosses her arms. "When I was a little girl mi mama would give me and my cousins mason jars. She would tell us to go out and catch the night lights and bring them back to her, because they were her favorite summer memory from when she was a kid." Rosa leans on the counter. "My mother was sick a lot of the time. There were many days she couldn't get out of bed. She was always tired and in a lot of pain. She loved the summer time no matter how much she hurt. We would bring her our jars after spending half the night catching the fireflies and she would line them up on her windowsill. Her eyes would light up as she watched them flicker and she would say. Mira, mi ja. Mira God's lanterns, shining just for me and for you. Aren't they amazing?"

His head hurts. What is Rosa talking about? "Are you telling me to go catch fireflies in a mason jar for Maddie to get her to like me?"

Rosa shakes her head slowly back and forth. "No. Eschucha me," she orders. "I'm telling you to be the jar that holds the flame that illuminates Maddie." She raises a finger in the air. "*You* be her joy and her laughter. *You* be the flickering light that calls her home."

He sits down on a chair. "That sounds like a lot. What if I can't be all those things for her?"

She pokes him in his chest. "Trust me. You already are. She

doesn't know it yet. Have some patience. You are all those things and more for Maddie. That's what love is."

He sits in silence. He eats his crepes and drinks his coffee. He glances up at Rosa one more time. "Are you sure you don't want to help me practice making fried pickles and French fries?"

She laughs. "And get in the middle of a family feud that's been going on forever? No thank you. I'm not going to lose business over picking sides. You're on your own, cowboy."

He gets out his phone and texts his mom to ask for the secret recipe for fried pickles. He thinks to himself as he waits, *it's time to get down to business. Summer nights, fireflies, and mason jars will have to wait.*

"Oh, why don't you just go back to your double-wide and fry something!"

- *SWEET HOME ALABAMA*

Twenty

Maddie whips out another tray of hand-cut potato wedges with seasoning in her mom's kitchen. She takes a bite. "This batch has to be better than the last, or I'm going to scream," she mutters. She takes a bite. She throws her head back and screams.

Seconds later, her bleary-eyed mom pops around the corner. "Maddie, it's six o'clock in the morning. What in the world are you doing up on a Saturday at this hour, screaming like a mad woman in my kitchen?"

She tosses the rest of the wedges back on the pan. "I can't get this right, mom. They all taste like crap. Mason French is totally going to win." She bites her tongue, but it's too late.

Her mom looks confused. She sits down at the table and stares at Maddie. "Why isn't there any coffee on?"

"Excuse me," Maddie asks. She's all butthurt because she can't figure out what happened to her overly concerned mom who should be comforting Maddie now, or at least flipping out over the fact that she uttered the last name of their bitter enemy in the family kitchen. Her mom groans. Maddie startles and jumps around. "Are you okay, mom? Can I get you any medicine?"

Her mom's eyes fly open. She glares at Maddie, and Maddie wonders if her mother is going through menopause. "Coffee,

Maddie. Make me some coffee," she says before laying her head on her arms. "If you're going to wake me up from a dead sleep by screaming like a maniac in my kitchen, the least you can do is make me some coffee," she grumbles once more.

Maddie opens the oven door and peeks in at another failure waiting to happen. She spins around. "Fine. But if I burn those wedges because I'm making your coffee, well, you at least have to try one."

Her mom turns her head on her bicep and rolls her eyes before closing them. "Whatever you say, daughter. Just give me my coffee."

She dances around the kitchen with the empty coffeepot. "Don't you want to know what kind of contest I have going with Mason French?"

"You mean the one where he's totally going to completely annihilate you?" Her mom's lack of confidence in Maddie is *kind-a* hurtful.

"Mom. I'm your daughter. You're supposed to pick me to win, Maddie whines unconvincingly.

Her mom giggles. "I would if Mason's family hadn't already laid claim to the best fried pickles in the state."

What? "Are you serious? You can't be serious. That was just like an exaggeration. You know how Mason is."

Her mom shakes her head. "No. I'm not exaggerating." She stares Maddie down. "I can't believe you don't know their history."

Maddie stops herself from slamming the fridge door shut when she pulls out the milk, but she's so annoyed. "Of course, I know their history, mom. I went over it myself in school. His ancestor stole our ancestor's fiancée on the boat ride to America."

Her mom coughs and looks slightly embarrassed. What is that all about, Maddie wonders? "Well, I'd say that score is even."

Maddie's head pops up from searching for, well, she doesn't know, because she just forgot. "What did you just say, mom?"

Maddie notices her mom looks caught and that she's waving

her hand in a swatting motion. "Never mind the ancient Mayflower history, Maddie, I'm talking about more recent history, like the 1980s."

Maddie leans against the counter and waits for the coffee to be done percolating. Her brain can't seem to focus because of a certain someone and his stupid lips and his stupid hands and this stupid contest that she finds herself involved in that she's pretty sure she's going to fail miserably at. She hates failure.

"Maddie," her mother barks her name.

She blinks. "What, Mom?"

"Do you want to know what I'm talking about or not?"

Maddie isn't sure, as she can't see how it's relevant to how she's going to take Mason down. "I guess," she mutters in a response that seriously lacks enthusiasm.

Her mom shakes her head again. "I can't believe you don't know anything about their prized pickles. It was like a big deal for this town. It kind of put us on the map."

Maddie's had enough of the mystery and the feeling she's missing most of the conversation that she's currently involved in. "What are you saying, Mom? Was it really that big of a deal?"

Her mom sighs. "I guess you were like three or four when it happened, so it makes sense you wouldn't know, but it's so weird. The French's fried pickles were the stuff of legends." Her mom leans back in her chair. "At least in this state, and a few states around us."

Maddie snorts. "*Legends*, Mom? Really? Didn't they just sell them here in a local café with like no competitor and maybe win a few prizes at the county fair?"

Her mom looks wide-eyed. "You don't know the half of it, Maddie." Her mom shakes her head. "Boy, Mason must be more humble than I thought," she mutters.

Maddie can't take any more of the suspense. "Tell me the other half, then."

Her mom leans in across the table. "I'll tell you what I know, but you can't tell anyone in the family." Maddie can't believe her mom is whispering. Maddie feels all mafia as she pulls up a chair to sit smack dab in front of her mother. She slides a cup of coffee in front of her in offering.

"Lay it on me."

Her mom rolls her eyes and holds up an index finger. "One time, Maddie, I was going to do the *unthinkable*. It was 1994. I was going to go and work for the enemy. I'd filled out the application and everything. They were going to hire me at the lowest position possible, but I figured I could work my way up, so long as I got a piece of the pie."

Maddie's ears burn. Her mother sounds like a whacked-out conspiracy theorist. "Who are *they*, Mom?"

Her mom's eyes widen, and she slaps the table. "The Frenches, Maddie. Who else would *they* be?"

Maddie's annoyed with her mom's outburst. She keeps quiet and waits for her mom to continue. Her mom pauses and raises her eyes to the ceiling. She sits really still in her chair. She looks all around like she expects the FBI to sneak up on our top-secret conversation. Satisfied they are all alone, she leans in again. "As I was saying I was going to start working for the French-fried Pickle Company, but your father found out and he put his foot down. It was the only time your father yelled at me. He got so mad at the thought of me working for the enemy he threatened to take my car keys." Her mom leans back in her seat and waves a hand over the back of her chair. "Like I was some sixteen-year-old girl living at home with my father and not a twenty-five-year-old woman who was grown and married."

Maddie's still confused. "Why did you call the café they ran 'the company'?"

Her mom sits up straight in her chair once more. "The Frenches started with a small dream of a café, but it was so popular, they soon decided to dream bigger. They opened a factory where they sold homemade pickles in a jar along with a jar of their special pickle batter, and it worked. People from all over the country bought their product. That product sold so fast they could hardly keep up." She shakes her head. "It blew up overnight. It was nothing short of a miracle." She wags her finger. "And this was before social media was like a thing."

Maddie contemplates all of this. "If what you say is true where's the factory now? Was it in our town?"

Her mom rolls her eyes once more. "It's still here. But now it's known as *The Flour Pot Bakery*. Katie and John run it. Katie makes the cutest cookies and the prettiest cakes. You've seen them. They totally remodeled the place. It's adorable."

Maddie's eyes narrow. She still has her doubts. "If the French's fried pickle business was so booming, why did it close?"

Her mom's eyes dim a little. "When Mason's great grandma passed in 1996 the café closed and it never reopened. Her husband couldn't do it without her." Her mom continues. She gets a faraway look in her eye. "The factory stayed open for another six months, but it just wasn't the same with her gone. It's like all the joy left with her. It became a dreary place to work. Everyone kept working, but they fought and grumped at each other. It slowed down the production. The billing department got overwhelmed. They were getting paid plenty, but the floor couldn't keep up with the orders, so they were having to send out refunds. The old man couldn't take all the stress. He shut it all down and it just never reopened."

Maddie clears her throat. "So, Mason is using the family recipe, but he's never made it himself. I think I have a fighting chance at this cook-off."

Her mom gives her a resigned look. "Maddie, I love you. You're a lot of wonderful things, but cooking isn't exactly your strong suit."

Maddie's back is up. "Mother. If you meant to inspire me to work harder with your constructive criticism in your loving motherly way, you have succeeded." She raises a pointer finger in the air. "I'm going to win the contest. You'll see." Maddie throws a hand on her hip. "That'll clear our family name once and for all. It will prove to everyone that Mason's family stole my family's recipe."

Her mom raises her eyebrows at Maddie. "If you say so. Personally, I think you'd have better luck reading a poem you wrote about fried dill pickles." She taps her fingers on the table. "So, how's your 'how we met' articles coming along?"

Maddie grins back at her mom. "Pretty good, actually. It's kind of fun hearing how our neighbors met their spouses."

Her mom laughs. "Neighbors, Maddie? We live in the country because your dad didn't want any neighbors."

Maddie shrugs. "I don't know. Technically, you're right, we don't live in town. And maybe it's because our community is so small, but I feel like everyone's my neighbor even if they're literally not." Maddie sticks out her tongue at her mom. "Besides, didn't Pastor Garen say just last Sunday that everyone is our neighbor?"

Her mom smiles and raises her coffee cup to Maddie. "That he did, Maddie. That he did." Her mom gives her a wink. "It's nice to know you at least had your ears on the sermon."

Maddie pulls out another tray of wedges. By the look of them, she dreads tasting them. "Nuts. Most of them are kind of black on top," she mutters to herself. She glances over at her mother. "What's that supposed to mean?"

Her mom smirks at Maddie. "If I didn't know better, I'd say your church eyes were full of Mason French."

Maddie blushes clear down to her roots. "What's with you not getting upset about me staring at Mason or running around with him?"

Her mom looks a little uncomfortable. "We've already had this conversation. I like Mason just fine." She smirks. "Besides, I know you, Maddie girl. You might have a little fun with Mason this summer, but you're not sticking around. Your heart's always been in the city for as long as I can remember." Her mom beams up at Maddie. "You're my wanderer. You've always loved adventure." She gives Maddie a wink. "I don't foresee that changing anytime soon."

Maddie whips around to place the hot pan on the top of the oven. Her hands are a little hot inside her oven mitts. "Yeah, I guess."

Her mom sips at her coffee. "Goodness. I remember the days

of being free and wanting to take on the world. They seem so long ago." Her mom laughs like she always does when she's dreaming about her husband. Maddie might find it sickening if it weren't so sweet. "The girls and I were all set to spend the whole summer of '88 camping under the stars and cruising as many highways as we could across the U.S," her mom says with a sigh. "We shared as many dreams as three naïve nineteen-year-olds can." She shakes her head and smiles at a memory only she can see. "And wouldn't you know, this little no-name Kansas town was one of the first towns we came to. Our car broke down on the side of a gravel road and here came your father along to fix it." Her bright blue eyes flash beneath her dirty blonde bangs. She stares into space over her coffee cup. "I took one look at your father's fiery red hair and chocolate brown eyes and I was grounded. That was it. I knew from the moment I saw him he was the one for me. He became my whole world."

Her mom giggles. "My BFF's Kris and Lacie thought I was crazy when I told them I was staying behind. They spent all night with me in Kris's car trying to convince me to go with them and come back for him at the end of summer, but I knew, Maddie. I knew I had to seize the moment." Her mom takes a deep breath. "So the next morning, they dropped me and my suitcase off at the local hotel and they went on down the road." Her mom takes a big sip of coffee. "Maddie." Her voice is secretive.

"Yeah, Mom." Maddie says with a sigh that matches her mother's. She's heard her parents meet-cute story so many times she can recite it in her sleep.

"I'm going to tell you something I never told anyone."

Whoa. Maddie's eardrums just went on high alert.

"Okay." Maddie waits in suspense and dread. She stares at her mother and wonders what she's been hiding. Maddie hates that she can't read her mom's expression. At all. *Please don't tell me you gave up a baby and I have like a secret brother out there somewhere.*

A sly grin pops out on her mother's face. "I know I always told you your father and I started dating a few weeks after we met, but I never told you that he had a serious girlfriend when I met him."

Maddie blinks. "What?"

Her mom looks down at the table. "Yeah. When your father stopped to help us, there was a girl sitting in his car waiting on him. She put her hand out the window. I saw the ring on her left hand, and I was devastated. I couldn't believe I'd just met the man of my dreams and he was already engaged."

Maddie doesn't know what to say. She can't find any words. She waits for her mom to continue, but she doesn't. "What happened next," Maddie croaks.

Her mom taps her finger on the table before she starts tracing the edge. "The very next day I got a job at the same place the girl in the car worked, because I figured that would be the fastest way to see him again and it was." She grins a little grin. "Boy, was he surprised to see me working there when he walked in." She bites her lip. "I was beside myself, trying to figure out how to get him alone. But then I got extra lucky because his girlfriend had to run home that day for a family emergency, so I took the only chance I thought I'd get." Her mom wiggles in her chair. "I didn't waste any time. I told him I needed help getting something in a closet. Once I got him in there, I shut the door. I told him I knew we were meant to be together and that I would love him more than any other woman ever could, and that I would wait for him."

Maddie's jaw drops at her mother's strange confession. "And that worked?"

Her mom raises her eyebrows. "We're married aren't we?"

Maddie can't believe this. "You were sort of a hussy, Mom. Geez."

Her mom giggles. "I don't see it that way."

Maddie studies her mother. "Didn't you feel rotten about stealing someone's fiancée?"

Her mom shakes her head. "Not bad enough." Her mom rolls her eyes. "Besides, I watched his fiancée for the next few days before they broke up or whatever. She was a big old flirt.

By the way she carried on, you'd never guess she was engaged."

Maddie coughs. "I guess that makes it less awful, but still, mom. That's so weird."

Her mom shrugs her shoulders. "It didn't take her long to find someone else after they broke up." Her mom sits back in her chair. "And now you know why Mason's mom hates me so much."

Maddie's ears burn. "Are you saying what I think you are saying? You stole Mason's mom's fiancée?" Maddie thinks about it some more. "But we're neighbors."

Her mom looks all sheepish. "It's not something I'm proud of, Maddie, and we bought our house first. They built their house next to us after we were already here. If you ask me, she did it out of spite. Even if she couldn't have him, she was going to stay close by."

Maddie sits down across from her mother. She heard all the rest of it, but she's stuck on the beginning. "But you wouldn't take it back either."

Her mom looks at Maddie like she's crazy. "Of course I wouldn't. I'm just as in love with your father as the day I married him."

Maddie holds up her hand. "Wait a minute. So Mason's mom was going to marry the mortal enemy too?"

Her mom shakes her head at Maddie. "No, Maddie. His mother wasn't a French until she married." Her mom raises a finger. "But I wouldn't be surprised if she didn't marry Mason's father because he was a French and your father's sworn enemy."

Maddie narrows her eyes. "I don't know, that's pretty spiteful."

Her mom sips her coffee. "Her fiancée dumped her a month before their wedding day. I'm sure she thought it would hurt him to watch her marry his enemy. All's fair in love and war."

Maddie shakes her head back and forth. "That's crazy. This whole thing is just crazy."

Her mom nods her head. "I know. Given my history with his mother I can't believe Mason would be making eyes at you."

Maddie giggles. "You sound just like Grandpa Dean."

Her mom nods. "That's alright. Your Grandpa Dean is a wise man."

Maddie smirks. "Yep." Maddie taps her mom's hand. "I'm guessing your meet-cute story wouldn't be the best one to put in the local newspaper."

Her mom laughs out loud. "Not unless you want to stir up a hornet's nest."

Maddie turns away from her mom and heads back to the stove. "It might be funny to us, mom, and I can't say his mother doesn't deserve it. She's so awful. But I couldn't do that to Mason." Maddie stares at the blackened wedges and almost feels sorry for Mason's mom. She glances at her mother, thinking she must have been a bitter pill to swallow for his mother. Maddie swallows hard. "No wonder his mom looks like she swallowed charcoal half the time," she mutters.

Twenty-One

Mason yanks the tray of fried pickles from the oven. He can't believe he's spending his spare time in his mom's kitchen on a Saturday. He peeks outside at the sun shining through the trees. He watches the leaves dance in the breeze. "Dang it. It's a perfectly good day to be out fishing and boating. Instead, I'm in the kitchen working like a woman, burning fried pickles and French fries. Stupid Maddie and her big stupid, kissable mouth," he grumbles.

His mom pops in the kitchen. "Hey, son. What's going on in here?"

He turns to smile at her. "Oh, you know. I'm just seeing if any of that creative cooking ability was passed down to me. I'm getting ready to challenge Maddie Dill in a cook-off."

Her face turns sour like she's been sucking on a dill pickle. "Why?"

He's confused. "Why what?"

His mom clears her throat. "Why would you challenge *that girl* to anything?"

He shrugs. "I don't know. It started off innocently enough, but then she said she was going to prove once and for all to the entire town that we stole her recipe, so then I said 'sure, why not. I'll beat you in a fried pickles and potatoes contest.'" Mason looks down at the cooking failure in the pan. "Now, I'm not so sure."

"If we stole a recipe from them, it serves them right. Her mother stole my wedding day," his mom bites out.

"Whoa, Mom. What the hell are you talkin' about?" Mason asks as he plops down in a chair.

"Relax, honey," Mason's father bellows from the den. His mom flinches at his dad's hollering in the house. "You got the better deal, anyway."

Mason's mind is spinning. He feels kind of dizzy. He puts his head down and looks up sideways to stare at his mother. He can't believe she was engaged before she met his father, or that his father knows what she's talking about. And that his dad is obviously okay with all whatever this mess is. Mason is so confused. His mom walks over to the stove. "I don't understand why you're going through all this trouble. Just let me have my personal chef cook them up for you that day. Then they'll definitely win."

Mason gets to his feet. "No. I can't do that. If I'm going to win this contest, it'll be because I followed the rules. I'm not cheating."

His mom rolls her eyes at him. "Fine, Mason. Don't get all grumpy with me. It was just a suggestion."

Mason groans. "I'm a grown man, mom. I will either win triumphantly or lose gracefully, but either way I'm going to do it. You can't have someone do it for me."

His mom pats his shoulder. "Well, don't say I didn't try to help."

"I've never said that. I'm merely pointing out I'm twenty-three-years-old and I don't need you to hold my hand." He holds in a groan, thinking he knows his mom loves him, but sometimes she can be a bit much.

His mother sighs again. "O-kay, Mason. Have it your way."

Mason returns to the stove to try again. He takes a bite of a burnt pickle. "Ooh. That's disgusting." He turns back to his mom. He's still in disbelief. He thinks he understands, but he has to be sure. "What do you mean she stole your wedding day?"

"Maddie's mom stole your mom's fiancée," his dad yells from the den. Mason looks back at his mom who appears slightly mortified. Mason can't believe it's true, even though he can see that it is.

Mason studies his mom as the emotion slowly drains from her face. He tries to wrap his head around the fact that his mom almost married Maddie's dad, which means they probably... He whips back around and looks at the oven. "I'm just going to work on the recipe some more."

His mom walks up behind him and lays a hand on his shoulder. He hates himself for it, but he scoots away from her touch. "Mom, this is a little too strange right now. I'm just trying to catch up in my head."

His mom moves her hand away. "I'm sorry, Mason. I didn't mean to make you feel awkward. I never meant to tell you." *But you did*, he thinks to himself *and now I can't unknow what I know.* "The whole thing was so awful. She swept into town and whisked him off his feet a month before we were to be married, and the rest was history." His mom studies him. He stays quiet. He doesn't know what to think. "Say something."

He clears his throat. "If you had stayed with him, he could be my father, and Maddie would be my sister." *And what I feel for Maddie isn't anywhere close to brotherly affection.*

His mother laughs. "Oh, Mason. Maddie and you are night and day. She could never be your sister. She's so fearless and brave." Mason blanches just a little as his male pride takes a beating.

He looks over at his mom. "And what am I, besides not fearless or brave?"

She tears up and pats his cheek. "You're my son, Mason, and I love you. So much." She scurries away. Mason waits until he hears her feet on the stairs. Mason shuts off the oven and walks into his dad's den.

Mason knows things are already awkward, but he has too

many questions. "So did you marry mom because she was previously engaged to a Dill?"

His dad tilts his head back slightly in his big recliner and looks away from the baseball game. "Does it matter why we got married, son? We've made a good run of it. Your mom was always a looker, and she seems to tolerate me. We have three wonderful children. Let it go."

Mason plops down on the couch. "Dad, this thing with Maddie and me..."

His dad coughs. "You need to let that go. Your mom would never forgive you."

Anger Mason didn't expect fills him. "But what if I can't? What if she's the one?"

His Dad laughs. "Mason. You always were a little too soft-hearted. Trust me, Maddie's something, but she's not for you."

Mason's insides burn. *What the hell does that mean? Why does everyone have so little faith in me?* "Why do you say that?"

His dad snorts and taps his fingers on his chair. "Mason, you're like this town, okay?" he holds up a finger. "Reliable." He holds up another finger. "Dependable." He holds up a third finger. "Stationary." He turns to me. "And those are all good things, okay? So don't think I'm insulting you, cause I'm not."

Mason shakes his head. "Read between the lines, Dad. I'm screwed."

His dad laughs out loud. He raises his finger. "That was a good one, son." He chuckles to himself again. "But seriously, hear me out." He clears his throat. "Maddie is a visionary. She's got big dreams, dreams way bigger than this town." He shifts in his chair. "All I'm saying, son, is don't be the one to hold her back. She's meant for so much more than that."

Mason sits back on the couch. "Dad. What if she's my dream?"

He frowns and stares at the floor. "Well, you might've figured that out before you made all these commitments to your grandfather. As it is, that kind of sucks for you. You're pretty much committed to opening a business here. You've signed all the paperwork down at the bank. There's no getting out of it now." His dad nods his head. "Besides, it's good you're sticking around. Your mom doesn't like your other siblings bein' so far away."

Mason sits on the couch feeling strangled by responsibility and the idea that he can have dreams as long as they meet his parents' approval, which basically means he can't have them. He stares at the side of his dad's face. He's lost in the ballgame on the T.V. *This is a bunch of horseshit. I'm gettin' out of here.*

Mason hops out of the chair, turns off the oven, and walks out the back door. He needs a day at the pond. "Maddie can have her stupid pickle prize. I don't want it. I just want her," he says to no one as he climbs in his truck to take a drive. "And if my parents don't like it, I don't give a damn."

MYSTERY COUPLE

A GROWN MAN IS HARD TO FIND

I saw my future husband for the first time in a small-town high school of sixty students. I was a junior and he was a senior. We never spoke a single word to each other, but in a school that size by the end of the year everyone knows everyone. Even though we never spoke, I noticed him because he was quiet, and he always looked a little bored; like he was ready for whatever came after graduation.

We didn't run into each other again until seven years later. I was out one night with my cousin when I ran into him. He asked me to dance, but I've always been a terrible dancer, and so I asked him to dance with my cousin. After that, he came back to my table and asked me if I knew who he was. I laughed a little and said, "Yeah, I know who you are." We visited for a little while and then we shared a slow dance or two on the dance floor before he left with his friends, but not before he got my number.

I thought he was a solid guy who had both feet on the ground, knew who he was, and exactly where he was going. He was someone I could plan a future with. On one of our first dates, we went to a jazz concert. We were in our twenties and probably the only couple there under the age of sixty, but we didn't care. We were just happy to be there together and enjoy the music. We had a wonderful time.

We've been married twenty-three years and time has flown by. Our three children love to tease us about being "old-fashioned" in our actions and our thinking, but that doesn't bother us a bit. We're a couple of old souls and we take it as a compliment.

- Maddie Dill
The Daily Chase

Twenty~Two

Maddie rides the ATV down to the over-sized pond. She needs a good swim and some silence to clear her head and all of its crazy thoughts. She rides as close to the dock as she can get before hopping off and stripping down to her bra and panties as soon as her feet touch the boards of the dock. She runs over the boards feeling crazy and free. She's miles from anyone. No one can see the lake from the gravel road up over the hill. She craves air nobody else is breathing. She hops off the end of the dock and swims around a bit before lying on the opposite side of the bank with her eyes closed, enjoying the sunshine. She startles when she hears a big splash. Her eyes fly open. It's Mason. She knows she should be mad at him, but she just can't.

He swims over to her and hauls himself up on the grass to stand over her. He flips his head around like a dog. His grey eyes roam over her in blatant appreciation. She knows she should be offended but she's not. She feels so lost. "Did you know my dad used to date your mom," she asks in a tiny voice.

"Yep. I heard that rumor."

"When were you going to tell me?" she continues.

He shrugs and wiggles his toes in the grass. "I could ask you the same thing."

"It's *so weird*," she said as she stares up at the clouds. "We could've been like siblings."

He flops back on the grass beside her in his knit boxers to stare up at the sky. He lays his hands on his chest and turns his head sideways to look her in the eye. "Incest is best."

She laughs out loud and pinches his side. "That's so gross. Why would you say that?"

He shrugs. "I don't know. I'm dealing. I just found out this morning."

She turns her head toward his. "Me too," she softly whispers.

He moves toward her. She considers it for half a second before turning her head away from his and staring back up at the sky. "It's so weird to think my mom made such a bold move on someone else's fiancée."

"Do you think she's a bad person," he asks..

She shivers inside at his question. "I don't want to think that, but you have to admit, it's kind of awful."

"I guess, but at least your parents are happy."

She glances at him out of the corner of her eye. "What's that mean?"

He puts his hands behind his head. His elbow bumps her face, and she moves over a hair. "I mean, I think my parents might have gotten married out of spite. That's more than a little disturbing. I think mom married dad because of his last name, and dad married mom as a slap in the face to your dad."

She feels bad at his words even though none of this was her fault. "Maybe but think about it. If you didn't know any of this until now, didn't you think your parents were happy?"

He groans. "Happy enough, I suppose. But now that I know it, I can't unknow it, and now I don't know how much of their relationship is real and how much is just putting on a good show for everyone."

She closes her mouth. She doesn't know what to say. "Well, there had to have been some love there. They couldn't stay together this long if there wasn't."

He snorts. "Have you *met* my father? He just needs taken

care of. If a woman did his laundry, made his supper, and had his children, she could resemble a fence post and he wouldn't care."

She hates the hurt in Mason's voice. She wishes she could cheer him up. "They're your parents and they love you. That's all that matters. Their relationship is their business, not ours."

He frowns. "Yeah, I know, but when my mom starts telling me who I can and cannot date because of her sad history, then their business becomes mine. She's not going to tell me anything about who I'm allowed to love."

The air just got a whole lot heavier. "Okay, Mason. Calm down."

He props himself up on one elbow and stares down at her. "No. I won't calm down. I *want* to be with you. But I won't be your sloppy seconds, like my dad is with my mom. I want to be your first in everything."

"You can't keep coming at me like this. I don't know what I want to do, or where I want to go, but I've got something in me that needs to see the world, and I can't do that if I stay here." She sighs. "That's the only thing I know."

"I know. I know you have your dreams. I get it."

She looks up at him. "You do?"

He nods. "Yeah, I do. I'm taking over my grandpa's business because he asked me to, not because I want to."

Realization registers in Maddie's fogged brain. "So you're buying him out because of family obligations?"

He nods his head. "Yep."

"Why would you do that? That business of his has to cost a fortune. You don't have that kind of money."

His stubborn face takes over. "I'm going to buy him out over time. It's an investment like any good business is."

Her heart breaks just a little. "Why would you do this, if it's not what you want?"

His eyes soften as he looks down at her. "Because that's the kind of guy I am. I'm dependable and reliable. I don't run away from responsibility." He says with a sigh. "My family needs me and it's nice to be needed." He scoots a little closer to her. He's so close she feels his hot breath on her ear. "And if I can't have what I want, then I might as well help a few people along the way, especially ones who have helped me and won't break my heart."

She bites her lip. She wants to look away, but she can't, not when Mason's looking at her like she's his whole world. "I wish I could say something to make you feel better, but I can't. What you're saying is right. You are all those things, and that's why everyone loves you. You're everyone's go-to guy and you're always there for people in need."

He sneers at her would-be compliment. "But not for you, because you don't need anyone." He lays on his back again. His hot breath leaves her, and she feels cold inside. "You're like that woman in your favorite movie, *Far from the Madding Crowd*. You're too stupid to see a good thing when it's staring you right in the face."

She can't believe he just called her stupid. She leans over him. "Mason French, I am not stupid. I may be stubborn and hard to love, but I am not dumb. And it's not a crime to have dreams," she grounds out.

He grabs hold of her and tugs her toward him. He doesn't stop until she's completely on top of him. His lips go for her neck and her jaw. They find their way to her ear. She's burning up.

"Maddie, let me in. That's all I'm asking. I think we could be something really special if you'd give us half a chance," he pleads. His hand is in her hair. He pulls her down again, but she was already on the way there. Maddie can't listen to his words anymore, or she'll never leave this pond. Her lips find his and its pure magic.

His arms fly around her and hold her tight. She can't think of anyone or anything but him. It scares her how much he feels like home. When their kiss finally ends, she lays her head on his chest and listens to his heartbeat. She knows if she listens long enough, it'll sound just like hers. Her head spins just like it does any time Mason is near. She thought she knew what she wanted, but once again, she isn't sure. Visions of the world and all it has to offer call to her, but so does Mason French. *Stupid love. It makes you feel so crazy,* she thinks while she tries to shove those ideas out of her head.

———

Mason lies beneath the most perfect woman he's ever known or seen, and wonders for the hundredth time why he's so transparent when it comes to Maddie Dill. Just like he wonders how many times he's going to spill his guts to her before he realizes she's not interested, at least not for the long haul. He recalls Rosa's words of encouragement. They sounded so right and so easy. Rosa made it sound like if he just told Maddie what he was feeling, she'd be right there with him. *Yeah, right,* he thinks. Pour your heart out to Maddie Dill and prepare to have it stomped on or swatted away like a pesky gnat buzzing in your ear.

She lies on top of him. Her head is on his chest. It feels so right. He stares up at the sky and wonders how can she feel all warm and cozy while she rips his heart out with no remorse? It doesn't make any sense. She's irresistible. When they're together like this she makes him feel that way too. Until she comes to her senses and remembers her big-time dreams, and the fact that he's just a country boy stuck in his hometown because of family obligation.

His mind runs in circles. It's dizzying. Is he staying out of obligation? Or is he staying because he can't handle being an invisible fish in a gigantic sea; something his ultra-competitive brother Max loves to tell him whenever Mason asks him about investing in Grandpa Steve's store so Mason can pay it off quicker. Mason frowns. Part of him knows Max tells him that so he can argue with Mason and distract him from making Max answer the question about funding. Mason frowns again as he also remembers the sad part. Max's strategy usually works. Max makes Mason so mad when he starts in on Mason about the idea that he won't leave his hometown because it's the one place he feels known that the conversation always ends there.

He shakes his head. "I've got dreams too," he mutters.

She moves a hair. She's so still he thought she fell asleep. "What are your dreams?"

He clears his throat. "I don't know exactly. Sometimes I think it'd be fun to have a shop in the city with, like, things I made out of old tools and stuff." He is so embarrassed. She's going to think he's crazy. Who makes art out of old metal?

"So is it art, or is it practical?" she asks.

He traces shapes on her back with his fingernails. "It's both. Art should always be practical. Why make something if it doesn't have a use?"

She giggles. "Well, then. Maybe I should stop making French fries and fried pickles."

He chuckles. "Why's that?"

She digs her cold nose into his chest hair just a little. "Because." Her lips brush against his chest and he almost comes unglued. "Because I'm a terrible cook."

He can't help but smirk. He knows how much that admission had to hurt her to say it out loud. He thinks he should let her worry about him beating her so bad. It would serve her right, but he can't.

He pats her back. "Don't sweat it. I about set the kitchen alarm off this morning trying to make fried pickles. My mom even offered to pay somebody to make them so I could pass them off as mine so I could win the contest."

She lifts her head. She lays her arms on both sides of his chest and rests her chin on her hands. "No way."

He nods his head. "Would I kid you about this?"

"So, what're we going to do? Have a contest to see who can make the worst fried pickles?"

He laughs. "Wouldn't that be something?"

"I can't believe neither one of us can make a decent fried pickle."

"Yeah. I even asked Rosa down at the café if she would help me with it. She said 'no, you have a college degree, you figure it out.'"

She sniffs. "Boy, somebody's bitter."

He stares back at her. "Nah. I don't think Rosa's bitter. She's completely happy where she is running the café. It was her dream. I think she just likes givin' me crap," he says with a grin.

"I can't believe you're giving up your dreams for your family."

Her words hit him like a fist to the gut. He nudges her off him and gets up. He jumps in the water and starts swimming. He looks back at Maddie, his unobtainable dream, who stands in the grass on the pond's edge in her bra and underwear, looking all fierce. He can't help but think she could sell burnt pickles to him all day long. "Hey, Maddie," he calls out.

"What?"

He finds his feet and walks closer to her, but he stays in the water. "What if we made them together?"

She wrinkles her nose. "What good will that do?"

He shrugs. "I don't know, but it's worth a try." Mason warms to the idea. "Something in my gut tells me they'll come out awesome. Besides, we can't let the people down. It's already been advertised. It's out there. What have we got to lose?"

She gets a gleam in her eye. "We could make them together and then divide them and then see how everyone votes. That might be fun."

He groans. "Why would that be fun? Don't you realize if you trick everyone, they'll never trust you again?"

She eyeballs him. "Let's just call it a study in human behavior." She bites her lip. "No one will have to ever know we tricked them. I won't tell if you won't."

He laughs out loud. "Whatever. Whatever the outcome of this contest, you won't be able to keep your mouth shut, especially if you lose. You've never been a good loser."

She frowns at him again. "I can handle losing. I won't say a word."

His stomach churns at the thought of tricking everybody, but on the other hand, it'll be fun to spend some time in the kitchen with Maddie. He's curious to see why her French fries were so bad, and maybe she can give him a hint about his disgusting pickles.

"Alright, fine. It's a deal. I'll keep the secret between us. I suppose if no one finds out it's not hurting anyone."

Her smiling face is full of triumph. "You've got yourself a deal." Her smile leaves as fast as it showed up. "Aren't you worried about what your mother will say?"

He frowns again. "I'm a grown-ass man. If I want to make fried pickles with my mother's sworn enemy, I will."

She snorts again. "Yeah, okay, Mason. I'll believe it when I see it, and not a second before."

He flinches a little at her skeptical tone. "Why you need to be so judgy and so rude?"

She sniffs the air. "I'm not rude. I'm just being honest. I know your mother can't stand my family or the idea of me and you doing anything together."

He knows this is all true, but he's got his own life. Mostly. "I learned a long time ago pleasing my mom is a full-time job, not to mention impossible. And I'm done applying. So there."

She laughs out loud. "Sure you are. Now go tell that to your mother."

He ducks as he clears his throat. "She'll just have to get used to us being friends, 'cause you're my new cooking partner." He stares at Maddie, and she stares right back. Mason swears those eyes of hers could light him on fire. He swallows hard and hopes they don't burn down the kitchen. He coughs again. "But we're cooking at your house," he adds.

Maddie laughs out loud. "Way to stand up to your mother. That'll teach her," she taunts.

He hits the water with his hand. "Shut up, Maddie, or I won't be cooking with you," he threatens.

Mason can't believe his ears. Maddie's only response is to jump in the water and start swimming.

Twenty-Three

Maddie looks over at Mason. Her eyes widen. "I feel like I'm in the Twilight Zone. Mason French is in my kitchen and my parents are home. They've even walked through a few times and everyone was civil. It feels like Hell has frozen over."

He rolls his eyes. "Are you done now? Can we get back to work, please?" he asks as he measures out the dry ingredients. "Watch that oil you're heating. It has to be just right," he warns. Maddie feels his eyes on her. He makes her twitchy. "Careful, Maddie. If you heat the oil too fast you'll ruin the pickles."

She sighs a dramatic sigh. "Go jump in the lake, Mason. I think I know how to fry my own oil."

He steps into her space. His breath falls on her ear. "You know how to fry my oil too."

She gives him a shove. "Get back to your mixing, you kitchen perv."

He chuckles behind her, and her butterflies pick up their speed. He steps off. Maddie spins around and looks at his mixing bowl of dry ingredients. "That's not stirred up enough. The materials need to mix together completely or you're going to have half of them tasting like salt and pepper and the other half tasting like cayenne."

He snorts and stirs it some more with a fork, scraping the

side of the glass bowl. It goes off in her ears like fingernails on a chalkboard.

"Ugh. Stop using the fork. I hate that sound," she all but shrieks.

He laughs and scrapes the fork on the bowl some more. "You mean this sound?"

She dashes over and rips the fork from his hand. She gives him a rubber whisk. "Here. Use this."

The oil pops in her ear. "Crap balls. The oil's getting too hot." She reaches over and turns the burner down before she looks back at Mason. "Hurry up and dredge those pickles so I can fry them."

He makes a face. "What the heck does that mean?"

She rolls her eyes. "Stick a fork in the pickle. Then drag it through your dry ingredients so I can toss it in the hot oil."

"Oh, okay," he answers and does what she asks before tossing the pickle at her. It hits the side of her frying pan and slides down into the oil. He grins. "Basket, two points."

She frowns at him. "You got lucky. Don't be throwin' pickles in my kitchen and makin' a big old mess unless you want to clean it up." He drags a few more through the mix and carries them over to the pan and drops them in the oil. They splat. A little bit hits her wrist. "Ouch, that's hot oil on my arm."

His eyes fill with alarm. "I'm so sorry. Go stick your hand under the faucet. I'll turn the pickles." He shoves her out of the way.

"Calm down. It's just a little grease. I'll be alright," she says as she runs cold water on her arm and stands back to watch him fumble with the pickles in the grease, but he doesn't. He flips them over so fast they don't have time to burn. A few seconds later, he plops them on the napkin-covered plate to cool off. She takes his spot and dips some more pickles in the mixture before dropping them in the hot oil.

He touches her arm gently. "Are you okay?" His question is simple enough, but it isn't. She doesn't know if she's okay, just like she doesn't know what she's doing in her mom's kitchen with Mason French. She can't believe the amount of emotions that want to flow out of her every time he's around. It's like she has a hidden fountain of repressed feelings inside, and he's the only person who can make it flow. "Does it hurt?" he asks. *Only when I'm near you.*

She's lost in thought. "Sometimes it does, but sometimes it's not so bad."

He looks at her like she's nuts. "Your arm."

She blushes over her confusion that he caught so quickly. "Oh, yeah. A little. It hurts a little."

He gets all serious. "Well. Sometimes a little pain is good. It reminds us we are all human."

She studies him. "Thank you, Socrates, for that life lesson. I'm just going to get back to playing with my pickles now."

It's a little awkward but before long, they get into a smooth rhythm, and their dill pickles come out nice and golden brown. There's not a burnt spot to be found. She's so happy. She picks one up and so does he. He raises an eyebrow. "Are you ready for the moment of truth?"

She exhales. "Yeah."

"One, two, three, taste," he says. They both take a bite. They can't believe it. It tastes just right. She turns to him with a huge grin. "Wow."

He looks right back at her. "Wow is right," he agrees as he leans forward and steals a dill pickle-y kiss that she mostly dodges. His lips land on the corner of hers. "I don't know if it's your kitchen or what, but these pickles are perfect!"

"I don't know about that. This the same oven I managed to burn a bunch of wedges in."

He makes a face. "Did you bake them?"

"Isn't that what you do with potato wedges?"

He nods. "I suppose but we could try to use a Fry Daddy instead."

She wrinkles her nose. "I hate Fry Daddies. There's so much grease. I think we should try baking them one more time to see if I can't get it right. They're healthier that way."

"It's a contest about taste. Who cares if they are healthy?"

She raises her hand. "I care, okay? I care. Too much grease

isn't good for anyone, especially all these elderly people who have heart conditions and high cholesterol. I'm trying the baking again."

She opens the freezer and whips out her precut potato wedges. "Here. I have some more. They're already cut and everything. I'll just turn on the oven and spray a few cookie pans and get them ready."

He tips her skillet sideways and drains all the grease into an empty tomato can. He moves the hot pan to a different burner. "So, Maddie, did you hear Merk the Jerk was getting married?"

"Yeah, I heard that from Alex." She shakes her head. "I can't believe he actually found someone to marry him."

"Yeah. Her name is Nicole." He chuckles and crosses his arms on his chest. "Apparently, the girlfriend he had in high school, the one we all thought he made up, was real. That was Nicole. They've been together all this time and now they're finally getting married. She really was from another school."

"More like from another planet."

He snorts. "Ease up. Maybe the Merk the Jerk has a sensitive side we've never seen."

She focuses on preparing her potato wedges. "Whatever. I'm working on these now. I want to be sure they're good and covered with oil and seasoning." She looks over at him once more. "To each their own, I guess, but I can't believe she waited seven years to marry the guy."

"What do you mean?" he asks. She tries to ignore the fact that he's so focused.

"All I mean is I would think after seeing a person for six months you either know or you don't know, if you're thinking long term."

"I can't believe you of all people would say that. He shifts his head to lean against the counter, crossing his ankles. "Weren't you engaged to Jeff for like two years or something?"

She fidgets. "That's different, though, because we were both committed to our career plans." She shifts her gaze. "Besides, he proposed to me after six months."

His heart pinches a little. He shoves away his hurt. "And?"

She frowns. "And what?"

"And what did you say?"

She looks down at the floor. "I said no."

He blinks. "He proposed to you more than once?"

She gives him a leveling stare. "You know me. Does that really surprise you?"

He chuckles. "I guess not, but you're the one who just said why wait seven years."

She rolls her eyes. "Well, that's different because obviously they knew each other if they'd been dating since high school."

He throws up his hands. "I give up. You win." She grins triumphantly. "So, Maddie Dill, the new relationship guru, what if the person you want to be with isn't thinking long term? How do you get them on the same page?"

She shrugs. "All I'm saying is, how long do you need to date someone before you know if they're somebody you can depend on, have similar goals and interests, be who you are with, and help you be your best self?"

He smirks at her before slowly leaving his post on her kitchen counter to swagger across the room until he's right up in her space. He leans on the island and stares down at her. His eyes linger on her lips. "Those are all very nice attributes, Maddie Dill, but what about love?"

"Hmmm," is all she can say as she stares into his grey eyes, getting lost in his five o'clock shadow that outlines his perfect jaw line so nicely. "I'm sorry. I forget the question."

"Love?" His voice is all rumbly and low.

"What about it?" she asks, all testy and flustered.

"All those things you named sound nice, but they sound like a check list or a job interview for the perfect roommate. What about sweaty palms, a nervous stomach, and a racing pulse?" he asks just above a whisper.

His sappy words and smirky face annoy her, because she feels them all. "Are you describing falling in love or an anxiety attack because I could go either way here."

He grabs her arm and pulls her up against him. She about

flips her potato wedge pan off the counter. "Watch it. You're messin' with my potatoes," she grumps.

"Well, you're messin' with me, Dill Pickle," he growls out before pulling her to him for a searing kiss. Maddie's toes curl inside her shoes. *He's so hot.*

A throat clearing startles them. Mason releases her. Maddie's father stands in the doorway. "Let me fall through the freaking floor," she mutters under her breath.

"Mason."

He tears his eyes from hers and looks over at her father. "Mr. Dill."

Her father winks at her. "Be careful tasting those spicy dill pickles, Mason. They have a wicked bite."

Mason swallows hard as he watches her father leave the kitchen. "I always liked your father."

Maddie turns away from him with trembling hands. "Yeah, he's a real comedian." She coughs. "I'm just not used to him making jokes at my expense."

Mason's hand falls on her shoulder. He gives her a squeeze. "It's okay. He probably didn't know what to say. You're his little girl." She spins around. She goes to speak but stops when she catches the hungry look in Mason's eye. He coughs. "I, uh, well before all this started, I meant to ask you if you would go to The Jerk's wedding with me."

She stares back at him and tells herself not to read anything into it, that it was just crazy timing, the kiss and then the wedding invite. It doesn't mean anything, really. She glances around the room, feeling more closed in by the minute. "This kitchen is too small for us both to cook in, and I knew that from the beginning. We just need more space between us, that's all," she muses.

Mason looks at her like he's hanging on by a thread. She can't tell him no. "I guess I could go to the wedding with you," she says a little too brightly. "I mean, I won't believe The Jerk's married until I see it with my own eyes."

He relaxes a little in his stance. Some of the heat leaves his eyes and he deflates. He takes a deep breath as if he's willing himself to breathe. "Alright, then. I'll just text you the deets."

She laughs out loud again. "Did you just say deets?"

"No, I um, I totally didn't say…" He stops talking. He nods his head. "Yeah, okay, yeah. I totally said that."

She giggles, but she's thankful for the break in the tension. "Well, alright then. I'll just watch for, you know, the deets," she answers and then snickers again.

He gets all embarrassed. "I was kidding, okay? Calm down about my outdated vocabulary."

The oven beeps at them, saving them both from any further awkward commentary. She grabs the potato wedge pan and sticks it in the oven. She sets the timer. She catches Mason eating more pickles out of the corner of her eye. She slaps his hand. "Hey. Stop eating those!"

He grins. "But they're so good. What are you saving them for, anyway?"

She shrugs. "I don't know, but I didn't make them for you to eat them all in one setting."

———

Mason chuckles. "I still can't believe Chad invited me to his wedding, Maddie. It's so crazy."

She rolls her big brown eyes. "Well, you said that he was a lot nicer when you saw him that night at the bar."

"Yeah, but he was drunk, so I don't know how much that counts."

She raises a questioning eyebrow. "And you have the invite?"

He gives her an affirmative nod. "I do. I even checked the name and address twice, because I still thought for sure Chad sent it to the wrong person." He taps a finger on the countertop. "I know it's all in the past, but it's pretty hard to forget someone who made me his favorite pinata day after day on the school playground, which is why I'm still not sure why he invited me to his wedding."

She pinches the top of her nose. "You don't have to tell me how awful Chad was. I was there."

He shakes his head as if he's lost in thought. "I know, but you have no idea how many times I've studied Chad's picture. I mean, it's too many times to count. I guess I was searching his freckle-covered, brat-faced persona for any trace of humanity."

She giggles. "I can't believe you did that. I mean, the best part of my school day was the end because it was Chad-less because he couldn't follow me home."

He laughs out loud. "As if you were afraid of that happening. I remember you teasing Chad so bad that you made him cry. Remember? It got so bad I had to ask you to get off his case." He stares her down. "You were ruthless."

She frowns. "The kid had a mouth that never shut up and he was so awful. I never could figure out why the girls thought Chad was so cute. He so wasn't. If a guy can be that awful, why can't a girl? Chad Merk got everything he deserved and then some."

Mason chuckles to himself. "I guess so. I still remember what you told me once you finally stopped harassing him. You said, 'some things I can never change, Mason, and I have to accept that. Chad will always be a bit of a turd and so I just need to learn to watch where I step.'" He gives her a wink. "You were wise beyond your years."

She looks sheepish. "Yeah, well. I s'pose it's confession time. My mom told me if she got called to the principal's office one more time because of me and Chad, she was going to home-school me."

His grey eyes widen. "No way."

She grins and raises two fingers. "Scout's honor. And then she told me what you just said, and so I just paraphrased a little. Mom always had my back. She didn't tell me I was wrong for giving as good as I got. She just gave me another point of view, one that wouldn't get me in so much trouble."

He smiles and shakes his head again. "I love your mom." He clears his throat. "Well, hopefully we can watch our step at Chad's wedding. Who knows what that's going to be like."

She frowns at him. "Oh, relax. The Jerk couldn't have found a woman who would put up with his ridiculous obnoxiousness. I bet she's reformed him and he's almost husband material by now."

He snorts. "Yeah, right. Chad Merk, my life-long playground bully has turned into a decent, nice, and understanding guy just because he met the right girl to settle down with? How do I know this whole wedding isn't some kind of hoax, with a hidden camera filming everyone's reactions when he doesn't show up at the altar?"

Her face goes beet red. "He'd better not stand up a woman who's waited seven long years to get married. That'd be a new low for even him." She pulls the potato wedges from the oven. They're golden brown. She throws up her hands in the air. "Score. Look at my gorgeous potatoes."

He laughs out loud. "*Our potatoes.* We made them together."

She gives an over-exaggerated shiver. "Yeah, I know it was a team effort." She looks back at him with resignation. "I guess you'll do for a cooking partner."

He pulls her to him for a side hug, being wary of the pan full of potatoes as they check them again. "I'd say we make a pretty good team, Maddie. We're like peas and carrots." He points to the pickles in one pan and fries in the other. "Or should I say pickles and fries?"

She pushes an oven-mit covered hand into his side in slow motion. "Shut up. You're such a cheeseball."

He grins down at her, thinking she makes him feel cheesy, and he doesn't even care. "The cheesiest," he says.

Her face turns red. He lights up inside at the thought of having made her blush. She moves away from him. "I'm going to get another pan of potatoes ready."

He reaches out, grabs a potato wedge and pops it in his mouth. "Hot, hot, hot," he says as he moves it around with his tongue and takes a slow bite as he hops around the kitchen. Steam hits the roof of his mouth. His eyes water. "I'm going to be peeling that skin off by tonight, but I can't help but smile.

The flavor of this potato wedge is the bomb," he manages to get out.

She rolls her eyes. "Why don't you just spit it out," she orders.

"I like the burn," he says.

"Suit yourself," she quips.

Twenty-Four

After a few more pans of potatoes wedges, Mason takes off for home with a container full of pickles and their version of fries. Maddie watches his truck back out of the driveway and shakes her head.

"It's a wonder this world didn't come to an end. I never thought I'd see that truck in our driveway." Her father's words startle her. She didn't hear him in the kitchen.

She turns to face her dad. "Yeah. Me neither."

Her father clears his throat. "So, Mason French, huh? Do you have any idea what his mother would do to you if she knew you two were 'Frenching' in the kitchen?"

She gives her father a shove. "That's so gross, Dad. Why'd you have to say that?"

Her father chuckles. "Hey, I call 'em like I see 'em."

She drags a toe across the floor. "O-kay."

"As I was saying, do you know what his mother would do?" her father scolds.

She stares back at her father. "I imagine you do, since you dumped her and all, a month before your wedding day."

Her dad about chokes on the potato wedge. "Yeah. You weren't really supposed to find out about that."

She makes a face at him and tilts her head to the side. "Maybe, but I did, so what's your version?" She watches her dad go to the cupboard and get a big glass. He fills it with water and drinks it down. She waits impatiently by the sink, tapping her fingers on the counter. He turns the faucet on again. She shuts it off. "Dad," she prompts.

Her father slowly turns to look at her. "I have one thing to say about the whole thing." She waits with anxious anticipation. His face is all serious as he looks down at her. "You've met your mother," he states.

She waits some more. She gets nothing in return. "Are you kidding me, Dad?" She whines. "And…"

He gives his daughter a wink. "She's a force of nature."

She rolls her eyes. "And?"

He throws out his hands. "That's all I'm going to say."

She slaps the counter a little too hard. Her palm stings. She thinks she'll probably have a bruise. "That's it? That's all you have to say? You dated his mother all through high school. You were going to get married. You were only a *month* away from your wedding day," she exclaims.

Her father nods. "Yep. But engaged isn't married. I married your mother, and I haven't regretted a single day we've been together, but I just might if you end up with Mason French." He winks at her and laughs from the kitchen doorway. "But if you do, you do, and I'll deal with it. You can't stop love, and something tells me you are your mother's daughter."

Her mom steps inside the doorway to lean on her father. She lays one hand on his chest and the other on his butt. Her mother gazes up at her husband with blind adoration. They make Maddie so uncomfortable sometimes. "Kiss me, dah-ling. I need some sugar."

Her father leans down and lays a noisy kiss on his wife. Maddie takes off in another direction. "I'm just gonna run over to Alex's. I'm taking the golf cart," she says as she walks out the back door of the kitchen and into the yard. She hasn't seen Alex in a while and she's not sticking around for her parents make-out sesh to escalate. Apparently, they don't realize they're middle-aged.

———

Maddie starts up Alex's back steps but stops when she hears Mason's voice.

"I just don't know what to do. She's driving me insane. I can't think when she's..."

She feels like such an intruder, but she can't listen to any more of this. Alex is her best friend too. She grabs the screen door and lets it go. It whaps against the house. She waits half a second before stepping inside. "Hey, guys," she announces. *Oh, boy,* she thinks. *I must sound like Miss Mary Sunshine because Alex is giving me a look of bewilderment.*

"Hey, Maddie," Alex answers from where she sits but she's grinning at Mason. "We were just talkin' about you."

Mason kicks Alex under the table. Alex grimaces and leans over to yank out one of Mason's leg hairs. His face goes beet red. "Ow!"

Alex sits up with a huge grin and winks at Mason. "Re-tri-bu-tion."

Mason leans back in his chair, still scowling. "You're a cold woman, Alex."

Trint drops a fist on the table. "How dare you. My wife is smokin' hot." He blows her a kiss.

"Puke," Maddie coughs into her hand. She looks around the room, feeling frozen in her tracks. "Should I leave, or..."

Alex shakes her head. "No, Maddie. You should *definitely stay.* Now we can play cards, like the good old days."

Maddie is thankful for a safe subject. "Sure. You got a UNO deck lying around?"

Alex giggles. "No. We play pitch or poker and we bet with pennies."

Maddie plops down in a chair. "I'm no good at either of those, but I'm willing to try."

Alex winks at Mason. "Remember playin' cards with Brittney?"

Mason shakes his head back and forth vigorously. "Please, Alex. Don't bring her up. I'm trying not to vomit over here."

Maddie looks between Mason and Alex and waits anxiously for more. She gets nothing. "Who's Brittney? Don't you think you're all being a little harsh? She's not here to defend herself."

Alex smirks at Maddie. "Brittney was a young single girl. She *loved* to play poker. She played it a lot, but she was terrible at it."

Maddie feels like there's something she should be getting, but she's not. "What's wrong with that? So she lost a lot of pennies; more for you, I guess."

Trint laughs. "More like clothing, Maddie. She lost a lot of clothing."

Maddie's instantly embarrassed. "Um. Why?"

Mason levels Maddie with a stare. "She *chose* to play strip poker. It was her favorite game."

Maddie's jaw drops at the thought of another girl getting undressed in front of Mason in this very kitchen. "And you played this game with her?"

Alex wiggles in her seat. "In his defense, Maddie, he asked her more than once to put her clothes back on or to at least slow down with her stripping."

"How noble of you," Maddie snarls at Mason, who keeps his pink-cheeked head ducked and wisely doesn't answer.

"Yeah." Trint smirks in Mason's direction. "He was noble alright. I never seen him have so many problems with his truck as when Brittney came around."

Mason slides down in his chair and ducks even further beneath his baseball cap. Maddie tears her eyes from shrinking Mason to look back at Trint. "What do you mean?"

Trint grins at her. "Brittney was forever trying to get a ride home with Mason, and most times she was about half dressed. But Mason here had the darndest time with his truck after dark. It seems his battery was always dead, so Brittney would have to find another ride home, because Mason was already out the door and walking by the second time she asked for a ride."

Maddie stares at Mason. "You live like seven miles from here."

Mason stares back at her. "It is 8.6 miles to be exact," he deadpans.

Maddie can't help but smile a little. "And you would walk that far just to avoid giving her a ride home?"

Mason rolls his eyes and picks up a card. "It's like Trint said. My truck was very temperamental. Don Quixote doesn't haul garden hoes," he quips.

Alex slaps her hand on the table. "I hate that word, and you know it, Mason. Don't you use it in my kitchen. You men are just as bad. It's such a double standard."

Mason lifts the bill of his hat to eyeball Alex. "I never gave her a ride home, Alex." He drawls. "Don't be yellin' your women's lib spiel at me." He looks over at Maddie. "Now, you going to be my pitch partner, or what?"

Maddie shrugs her shoulders. "I hope you like losing."

Mason's face is all serious as he peeks over his cards. "If I have to lose, Maddie Dill, I'll choose losing to you every time." Maddie's insides go sideways. She's not sure she can play any games with Mason without losing her heart.

Alex places a hand on her heart. "Oh, Trint. Remember when you used to talk sweet to me like that?"

Trint's jaw tightens just a hair. "I don't lose, baby. I only know how to win."

Maddie sticks a finger toward her mouth like she's gagging as she looks over at Mason. "Barf." Maddie glances at Trint. "Just for that comment, I might try a little harder at cards."

Trint sticks his tongue out at her. "Good. Winning feels even better when I'm challenged."

Maddie looks over at Mason sitting across from her. "You played cards with this big mouth, and you came back?"

Mason gives her a helpless look. "Well, I like playing cards, and this town is pretty small, so yeah."

MYSTERY COUPLE

LOVE IS PATIENT, LOVE IS KIND

I met my future husband at work. I was a second-year teacher at a small-town high school, and he was the new teacher. The school secretary had already scouted him out for me, so to speak. She only had good things to say about him when we visited about the new guy.

He was very easy to be around, something I noticed right away, and we quickly became good friends. I was drawn to his honesty and straight-forward manner. It was during our friendship that I really got to know him, and I liked everything about him.

Neither one of us was in a big hurry to jump into the deep end. We took our time getting to know one another. We dated for a year before getting engaged, and then we were engaged for another year before we were married. He kept his sense of humor through it all even when I asked him to change his hairstyle.

We've been married for twenty-six years. We've faced a few tidal waves but for the most part it's been smooth sailing, and I wouldn't choose anyone else.

- Maddie Dill
The Daily Chase

Twenty-Five

Mason shifts a little uncomfortably in his chair at Alex's table. Trint explains the game to Maddie, but Mason is lost in thought. He pounds the table and points an accusing finger at Alex. "I can't believe you brought up Brittney, the stripper."

Mason pauses before pointing at Maddie. "And I can't believe you are giving me the evil glare that I so don't deserve." He leans back in his chair, staring the two women down. "Doesn't it count for something that I never came close to doing anything about her other than run away?" He eyeballs Alex hard. "Brittney was your friend anyways. It's not like I invited her to our card night." He turns to Trint. "Tell me we weren't all relieved when Brittney left town after hanging around for a year, which, by the way, was one year too long." He coughs. "I think she had serious intentions about finding a man, but she went about it all wrong, or at least she was too forward for me." His eyes fly to his cards. "I swear. The last time I saw her, she practically chased me down your driveway in her bra and underwear. It was so awkward. I didn't come back here for like two months."

The whole kitchen goes quiet. Trint glances over at Mason. "Are you done with your rant? Are you ready to play cards?"

Mason holds up his cards in front of him. "You dealt me an awful hand, Trint. I want a do-over."

Trint smirks. "Heck, no, Mason. My cards look pretty good."

Maddie kicks his shin under the table. "No cheating, Trint. If you cheat to win, it doesn't count."

Trint rubs his leg. "Damn, Maddie. You have a hard kick."

Mason stares at Maddie across the table. "Tell me about it," he mutters. Maddie gives him a look that makes him go back to staring at his cards, but his concentration is shot. How can he play cards with Maddie? All he's thinking about is this wedding they're going to and what she's going to wear, and how gorgeous she'll be in a dress and how he's going to use the wedding date to his full advantage in taking their relationship to the next level.

Trint clears his throat. Mason blinks. He thinks he's been starin' at Maddie this whole time. That's not awkward. Maddie winks at him. "Hey, Mason. Remember that time we went *clubbing* and the bodyguard wouldn't let us into the *club*?"

Mason searches his memory. "No, I never went anywhere with you because you didn't talk to me in your college days."

Trint snorts. "I think she just told you she's got a good hand in *clubs*."

Maddie's face flames. "Well, that went over like a ton of bricks."

"It's not my fault we didn't go clubbing," Mason mutters in response.

Maddie rolls her eyes. "Mason. We're not talking about the past tonight. We're playing cards."

"Well, maybe I want to talk about it." Mason stares at his cards.

Maddie can't believe he's doing this in front of Alex and Trint. It's so dumb. Mason thinks he may as well be Walter Matthau from *Grumpy Old Men*, rehashing the past. Maddie clearly doesn't want to talk about it, but he still waits for Maddie to respond to his comment. She doesn't. He clears his throat. "Apparently, I'm the only one who's wounded by our friendship ending so abruptly."

Maddie throws her head back and growls. "It happened *seven* years ago, Mason. Those days are long gone. You can't get them back." Her head flops back down and she faces him straight on. "What do you want me to do about it?"

Mason shrugs. "I don't know, but you could at least try harder to act like you're sorry."

She tosses down her cards on the table. "I'm *not sorry*, Mason, okay? We talked about this already. You made a move on me, and it wasn't welcome. Everything was awkward after that, and our friendship was ruined. There's just some things you can't undo." Maddie snatches her cards back up.

Trint coughs. He opens his mouth to speak. Alex shakes her head at him. He closes it again. Trint looks over at Maddie and her self-satisfied smirk. He lays down his cards. "Actually, you should have seen it coming. Any straight man who has a girl for his best friend in high school, either wants to sleep with her, or..." he pauses and shakes his head. "There's no alternative. He wants to sleep with her. Us guys really are that simple."

Maddie's eyes narrow. "No, Trint, it isn't. Not everyone is a perv boy like you."

Mason coughs. "I agree with Trint. It really is that simple."

Maddie slaps the table. "Well, of course you agree with Trint since he's totally taking your side and you idiots have to stick together."

Alex grabs Maddie's wrist. "Don't call my husband an idiot."

Maddie moves away from Alex. "Why not? You call him an idiot sometimes."

Alex makes a face. "Of course I do, Maddie. He's my husband and my idiot. You want to call a guy an idiot, get your own husband."

Mason grabs the side of Maddie's chair before it shoots up in the air like a volunteer for the job. *"Yeah, Maddie."* He mimics. *"Get your own idiot husband."*

Maddie jumps out of the kitchen chair. "Y'all are gangin' up on me, and I'm not havin' it. I don't have anythin' to explain to anyone here." Her gaze falls on Mason. "Especially not to you,

you connivin' manipulator. You came in here and got my friends to gang up on me, so I'll date you, well screw that. You can find another date to Merk the Jerk's weddin', 'cause I'm not goin'. At least not with you," she states before she marches out the back door.

"What does that mean?" Mason hollers through the window at her.

Maddie turns around and yells back at the closed screen door. "It means what it means. I'm goin' solo," she yells.

Mason ducks back inside the open window. "Maddie's going by herself to a wedding. That's nothing new."

Trint chuckles and shakes his head. "Boy, when you screw up, Mason, whew. You screw up bad."

Mason sits back in his chair with his cards. "I'm not a boy. I'm a man and now we can't play cards because I lost my partner."

Alex winks at him. "You could bid blind."

Mason shrugs. "Sure, why not? I'm already livin' on the edge by tryin' to talk to Maddie and get her to go to a weddin' with me. I might as well as shoot the moon."

Trint frowns. "I hate it when you do that."

Mason smiles back at him. "I know, but it's probably the only time I'll have the upper hand. I already called it, so you have to give it to me," he says as he reaches for the rest of the cards.

Twenty-Six

Maddie pokes along in her dad's golf cart, taking a back road. *Stupid Mason. Why does he have to be such a girl? Why's he making me bring up things in his past that obviously upset him? I don't know why it's my fault that happened. It's not like I wanted to talk about how our friendship ended. Again. In front of an audience. I'm not the one who brought up any of that. It was all him, and he's beatin' a dead horse by makin' me talk about it more and more and more. The past is the past. It can't be changed. I don't want to talk about it. And I stand by what I said. If he hadn't made a move on me, things might've been different. We could've stayed friends. I could've been his lab partner in biology and chemistry all through high school.*

Maddie keeps her foot on the gas, bumping along. *As it was, I had to work with Arthur, the brilliant exchange student from Russia, who knew everything about science but nothing about small talk or the English language. He's the first guy I've ever known who literally thought having a big brain and spouting off about it 24-7 is a turn-on. No one cares about the difference between electrons and neutrons inside an unstable ionic bond in outer space except a super-genius chemist, and that excluded the majority of our senior class.*

Maddie pulls into the driveway but then she backs right back out. She needs her peace and quiet, and she knows the best place to find it. She finds herself driving back to the little pond, staring out at the water, and remembering the last time she was here. She was in her underwear when Mason showed up. They had a very nice time. It was so relaxed, well, until he kissed her. Then she kissed him back and then she accused him of giving up his dreams for family obligations.

"Why do I have to be so hard on people?" she wonders out loud. "I so don't want to be. Besides, Mason's just being a nice guy. What's wrong with that? Nothing, except for the fact that he's staying here, in our hometown. Forever." She twiddles thumbs. "And I am not."

She tries to think of a way out for him from his family business, but she can't. Maybe it's for the best. As her mom loves to say; "we can't all just go around doing whatever we want with no consequences. Everything has a consequence."

She thinks out loud some more. "But you stole someone's fiancée, Mom, and where's your consequence? You have a happy marriage and a happy life." Maddie is sure she must look crazy sitting out by the pond in the dark having a conversation with herself, but what does it matter? There's no one to see her.

She stares out at the water some more. She wants to jump in and cool off. So bad. *But it's dark, and what if something happens and I can't get out? No one knows I'm here. It would be irresponsible of me to go out there* "So instead, I'll sit in my cart and stare up at the moon and wonder what I'm supposed to do with my life." Her phone lights up.

> Maddie. Come home, please. I need
> help. Mom.

Her mom's words fill her with panic. She puts the golf cart in reverse and heads for home. Her mind races. She prays a silent prayer. *Please God, let her be okay.* She returns to chastising herself. *Why did I drive clear out here to be alone? I could have sat in my room and stared out my window. If I did that, I'd be with my mom right this second.*

Minutes later, she whips into the driveway and almost hits the back of Mason's truck. She jumps out and runs to the front porch. She takes the stairs two at a time, rushing inside and heading for her mom's bedroom. Mason's carrying her mom to bed?

"Where's Dad?" she calls out. Her mom waves Maddie over furiously behind Mason's back like he can't feel her hand flapping around like a bird's broken wing. "What the heck is going on here?" Maddie yells.

Mason sets her mom down like she's made of glass. She reaches up and pats his cheek with her hand. Maddie stops in her tracks at her mom's antics. "Thank you so much. I don't know what came over me. I just felt so weak." Her mom's eyes fly to Maddie's. "Maddie, dear. Thank goodness you're here. Be a dear and bring me a cup of water, would you please?" Maddie gives her mom a look from behind Mason's back that she hopes conveys, *Sure, Mother, let me just throw it on you to cool you off.*

Maddie moseys out of the room as slow as possible. She figures since her mom and Mason are best friends now, they can visit all they want. Her dad walks in the back door shaking his head. "That was weird. Your mom told me we're out of dog food. I know we have a whole extra bag, but she was so insistent. I left the house and drove out by the cemetery instead. I'm not driving over to another town at nine o'clock at night for dog food."

Maddie gives him an exasperated look. "Mason's in the bedroom with mom. He's putting her to bed. She called both of us."

My dad leans against the counter and gives her a measured look. "Oh."

Maddie sighs. "Yeah, oh."

Maddie pats her dad's shoulder. "You know what? I'm just gonna head back out to the pond and think some more. That's where I was before mom texted me with her cryptic plea for help and sent my anxiety through the roof."

Her dad smiles his little grin. "At least your mother is okay this time."

Maddie makes a face at her father. "She's okay for now. Just wait until I get through chewing her butt."

He laughs. "Careful, Maddie. Your mom knows how to bite back."

Maddie steps out the door. "I know, Dad. I know. Where do you think I learned my vicious ways?"

Her dad chuckles. "Touché'."

Maddie steps outside. The pond is calling.

———

Maddie's mom lies in front of Mason on her pillow. She looks a little tired and a whole lotta sheepish, he thinks. Mason turns to see the reason. Her husband stands in the doorway, and he looks slightly amused.

"You wanna hop off the side of my wife's bed?"

Mason stands up and doesn't say a word. He isn't sure what to say.

"I apologize, sir. Your wife called me," Mason stutters as he stands up to walk past him.

Maddie's dad coughs. "I'm sure she did."

Mason walks around him to give them both plenty of space. "I'm just gonna go then, Mr. Dill. Goodnight."

Mason stumbles down the hall feeling weird.

"Mason," he hollers.

Mason doesn't want to go back in there. "Yeah," he answers.

"I think Maddie's out by the pond again."

Mason can't hide his smile. "Thanks."

Mason runs out the front door, but not before hearing Maddie's dad's low voice coming from the bedroom. "You up for a little rumble in the jungle?"

Mason blushes at her telling laughter.

"No wonder Maddie's always out of the house," he mutters as he heads for the pond. "At least my parents show some sort of restraint." Mason pulls up to find Maddie sitting on the front of the golf car, staring up at the moon. She turns toward him.

"Mason. Back your truck up here. I want to lie in the back and look at the moon."

Mason does as she says, mostly out of relief that she's still talking to him after the stunt he pulled at Alex's house. He pulls a pillow and blanket out of his back seat. He tosses it in his truck bed and helps her climb up in it. Mason remains on the grass. Maddie's mood's been all over the place lately. He has no idea what she's thinking now. She looks over at him. "Aren't you going to join me?"

Mason climbs over the back of the truck bed and lays down on the blanket beside her. They share a pillow as they stare up at the moon together. "What you thinking?"

She sighs a big sigh. "I'm thinking I haven't figured out yet how to not let my temper get the best of me."

He laughs out loud. She raises a hand. He reaches up and threads his fingers through hers before wrestling her tensed arm back down between them. "Take a deep breath." Her chest rises and falls. He tries not to laugh again. She's like a charging bull. "Breathe slower."

"I'm trying," she growls.

Her hand squeezes his. Mason can't help but notice she's got quite the grip strength. "Dang, Maddie. Have you been milking cows or what?"

She turns to look at him. "What?"

"You're cutting off the circulation in my fingers."

She frowns. "Let go of my hand, then."

"I like holdin' your hand."

"Mason, you're such a girl."

He bristles at her comment. "Well, one of us has to be."

"What's that supposed to mean?"

He considers his words. "It means you could try a little harder to embrace your feminine side."

She shrugs. "I'm a tomboy. You know this. I've always been a tomboy." She nudges him. "You're emotional enough for the both of us."

He hates that his feelings are hurt so easily. "Whatever, ice queen."

She pulls her hand from his. "I am not the ice queen."

He snorts. "Yes, you are. You have like no emotion about anything."

She shakes her head. "Just because I don't wear my heart on my sleeve does not mean that I don't have emotions."

He turns on his side to look at her. "Maddie, what are we doing?"

She side eyes him. "If you'd shut up long enough for me to talk, I'm trying to tell you I'll go to the wedding with you."

He clears his throat. "What if I already have a date?"

Her eyes widen. "Do you?" He is way too satisfied by the panic in her voice.

"No. Relax. I haven't even asked anyone else. I wouldn't do that to you."

She nods. "Oh, okay. Well, if it's cool, I'll go with you." She fidgets with her hands on her chest. "'Cause you know, it's a lot easier to go with someone to a wedding. Otherwise, you worry about who might try to take you home, and all that." Her voice drops off.

He smiles at her awkward explanation. "Definitely. I'm sure that's your first worry, since you've always had trouble telling people no."

She smacks his shoulder. "So, I'm a girl with principles and I'm kind of judg-y. So what?"

He grins full out. "I know. That's one of the things I like about you."

Her face is full of doubt. "Really?"

He nods his head. "Yeah, 'cause that just means when you've made up your mind about someone, you're not changing it."

She looks nervous. "So that means you're going to let me go with you to the wedding?"

He makes a face. "I guess. I mean, I was all ready to go alone and face The Jerk as a single loser guy with no date, but I think we could have some fun." She whips out her phone. "What are you doing now?" He watches her fingers fly. "I'm RSVP'ing."

He blinks. "Isn't their wedding like in two days?"

She giggles. "Yep."

He stares up at the moon. "Here's to procrastinating."

She holds her phone in the air as she types in our information. "I'm sending it. He can take it or leave it."

He laughs again. "Are you kidding? He's Merk the Jerk; of course, he'll let us in. How many people do you think will actually come to his wedding?"

She looks thoughtful. "I suppose you're right. I mean he's got to be desperate if he's inviting classmates, he hasn't seen in like five or six years."

"Did you get an invite, or were you responding to mine that I forwarded to you?"

She feigns looking all clueless. "I'm sorry, what?"

"You didn't get an invitation to his wedding."

She swallows hard. "You don't know that."

He chuckles. "So, he didn't invite you. "

She sticks her little nose in the air. "It doesn't matter because I'm going with you."

He stares up at the moon. "So you don't want me to warn him." He knows he's being ornery, especially since Chad told him to bring her.

Her nose goes a little higher, and he didn't think that was possible. "Warn him about what? We're grown-ups now. The Jerk should be able to handle whoever comes to his wedding."

He snickers as he remembers every encounter between Maddie and The Jerk. "Maddie, all I'm saying is, I probably need two hands to count the number of times you made him cry."

She elbows Mason. "That was a long time ago, Mason. We're grown-ups now."

He chuckles again. "You keep saying that, but we'll see if it's true."

Twenty-Seven

The second Mason and Maddie step inside the church for the wedding, Maddie realizes this was all a huge mistake. She glances over at Mason who's been strangely reserved from the time he picked her up until now. Maddie can't shake the feeling that there's something about today that makes her feel too much like she's stuck in a dress rehearsal for being the future Maddie French or something.

She knows it's completely unfair to Mason, but panic has set in, and she feels powerless to stop it. She feels like her whole life flashed in front of her. She can totally see their Victorian-style house, the one that sits on the corner of Union and Second, that is currently inhabited by Ms. Killeen and her questionable number of cats that rests just below an anonymous phone call to PETA.

She cringes at the thought of the white picket fence and her name on a stone, with their four children running around the house, being chased by a beautiful red retriever named Amelia, her one exotic allowance in their picture-perfect postcard life. She sighs as she envisions their smiling, happy, complacent faces. She is exhausted by her restlessness even though she is powerless to stop it.

She glances around the room, wondering why she can't be satisfied with a life like her mother's? Her mom moved from a bigger city to their small town without a backwards glance because of Maddie's father. She glances to the side and considers Mason. She can't help but wonder, is it because he's not enough for her that she's still searching? He stands beside her, smelling good and looking handsome in his dress clothes. Any girl would be beyond lucky to have him, so why isn't he enough for her? She feels uncomfortable because she's starting to think Mason isn't the problem.

She glances at the pews up front. Merk the Jerk's family mostly look normal, save for the man at the end of the pew with his baseball cap on backwards and a big smirk on his face. He thought wearing a thermal shirt was going to pass for dress clothes as he gives every girl in the audience who meets his eye the once-over, including her. She looks somewhere else. Doesn't he know that's what you wear to the rehearsal dinner and not the wedding?

Mason's hand snags her elbow and fire shoots up her arm. "Maddie, we need to sit down."

She follows him blindly up the aisle. She's stunned to see so many of their high school classmates here. She wonders if they came out of the same curiosity as she did, to see if Chad would actually show up on his own wedding day or if he's pranking them all one last time.

She pastes on a smile and sits down beside Mason. She barely gets comfortable when Josie leans forward with a big grin on her face. Maddie tries not to scowl, but it's hard. Josie's always in everyone's business. "So, are you two, like together?"

Maddie opens her mouth to speak, but Mason leans toward Josie while putting one hand on Maddie's hip and the other on her shoulder. He starts stroking her skin with his finger absentmindedly, driving her nuts. She forces herself to sit still and concentrate on what he's saying.

"No, Josie. We're not together. We just ran into each other this summer and it was explosive, so we're seeing where it goes from here." He coughs. "You know Maddie and her running shoes. She can't sit still long enough to stay anywhere very long." Mason's voice sounds resigned and pitiful.

Maddie's blood boils as she thinks to herself, *if this weren't a church, I'd punch him out.* Josie looks confused.

Mason clears his throat. "Anyways, I'm sure you heard by now, I'm buying out my grandpa, so it looks like I'll be staying close to home for the family and all."

Josie nods her head. "Well, that's just so sweet. It's nice to know some of us still know what family duty means." Josie gives Maddie a dirty look. Maddie smiles sweet as saccharine back at Josie, noting her tiny bulge which wouldn't be notice-able if she weren't wearing a dress as tight as a second skin.

"Speaking of family, Josie, are you expecting?" Maddie asks as she smiles all teeth at her.

A look of panic crosses Josie's face as the guy beside her tenses up tighter than a coiled spring about to pop while he stares at her stomach like he's waiting for it to come clean. Josie crosses her arms over her microscopic bulge.

"No. No I am not." Maddie feels a little bad about the guy's expression. She's pretty sure they'll be having it out later today. Josie looks like she wants to rip Maddie a new one, and Maddie's right back in high school.

Maddie tries to look contrite. "Oap. My bad." Josie scowls at Maddie and doesn't answer. Maddie spins back around. *Ha! That'll teach her for gettin' in my business. What a busybody.* Mason frowns at Maddie but she stares straight ahead. If he thinks he can guilt her into dating him, he's got another think coming.

———

Mason's ears burn. He can't believe Maddie Dill can be so rude. Okay, he can believe it and Josie probably had it coming, but still. Josie's comments weren't near as harsh as Maddie, who can't help herself from going for the jugular. Every time. Mason side-eyes Maddie in her sphagetti-strap deep purple dress that covers her knees. She almost looks elegant. Her styled hair and killer heels suggest she's a very attractive woman. That is until she opens her mouth to reveal her prickly-as-pear ways which throw her right back to her teenage years. He's sure Josie is mortified. By the looks of things, she and her boyfriend are probably headed for a break-up.

Mason glances over at Maddie whose jaw is set and wonders what she's so mad about? He only told the truth. Yeah, he laid it on pretty thick, but that's how he feels, and sometimes Mason feels like Maddie's not hearing him when it's just the two of them. He figures maybe if she's embarrassed in front of their old "friends", she'll rethink going out with him more than once in a blue moon.

He holds in a sigh when he realizes this is not at all how he wanted the day to go. He side-eyes Maddie, whose resting-B face has shown up in full force. The wedding hasn't even started, and the two of them are back to being mad at each other. It wouldn't be so bad if they got to kiss and make up, but those are perks Mason's not allowed to enjoy. Mason frowns at his reality, which consists of walking around Maddie on tiptoe like she's made of glass. It's getting old. Mason glances at her once more. Maddie stares a hole through the front of the church.

There's a small commotion as Chad and the minister take their place up on stage. Mason can't hold in his grin. At least one mystery is solved. Chad is here. Mason studies Chad's face under the bright lights of the church, and he can hardly believe what he sees. Someone who looks like a nice guy, and not at all like the teenage bully who used to stick Mason's head in the toilet for fun or shove him in the girl's restroom every chance he got. Mason smiles to himself when he remembers the day Maddie got Chad by the ear and dragged him across the girl's bathroom floor. After that bout of humiliation, Chad never shoved Mason in a stall again.

The music starts and the wedding party walks in. Soon enough, it's the bride's song. Everyone stands. She glides by and Mason spies her over Maddie's head. Mostly he watches Maddie for any signs of appreciation or longing, anything to indicate she might take the plunge one day.

Maddie turns to Mason just as the bride steps up beside Chad and mouths "Merk the Jerk". Mason fights the urge to cover her mouth with his hand and prays no one else saw what

Maddie just did. They sit back down, and the ceremony begins. Before too long, Chad recites his vows, or rather chokes out his vows. He's crying like a little boy.

Mason feels Maddie's trembling before he sees it, but he knows what's coming. Maddie hides her laughter in her hands, but not very well. Mason can't believe the amount of inappropriate emotion Maddie's shown today. He tries to give her a break. She is his wedding date. He sits in the church pew all uncomfortable, thinking this is Chad's wedding day, after all, and he can't help but wonder if Chad wasn't a tad bit correct in not sending Maddie an invite. Clearly Chad's not the only emotionally immature one in the room.

Mason pinches Maddie's upper arm to make her stop laughing but it has the opposite effect. She doubles over and bites her hand. Mason holds in a groan. He can't believe he just made things a whole lot worse. Mason glances at the back door of the church wishing they could bail, but they can't even do that gracefully as they'd have to climb over at least four people just to exit the pew.

He mentally kicks himself as he prays he can wait it out. He can't believe he used to think Maddie's hysterics were cute, even if they did happen at the most inopportune times. Like the time the class hamster was found belly up in his cage after a long weekend and rigor mortis had already set in. The whole class was horrified, but Maddie stood in front of the cage giggling like crazy before she finally got out, "he's stiff as a board," after poking him with a pencil through the cage to "wake the zombie hamster that would come for them in their sleep." Maddie always did have an overly active imagination, one that certainly wasn't fit for most second graders. He could tell from the quivering lips a few of their classmates believed her warning about blood-sucking zombie hamsters.

Mason couldn't believe the look of glee in Maddie's eyes as she went on about the hamster coming back to haunt them. He cringed as she told everyone they'd better all have a wooden stake close by in case the zombie showed up in their rooms. He was never so thankful as when Mrs. Wilhit showed up with her ever-practical manner of speaking. "Now, class, everyone here knows that there are no such things as zombie hamsters, right?"

To which Maddie responded just as quickly. "That's what she wants you to think." And then Mrs. Wilhit promptly walked Maddie to the principal's office.

Mason pats Maddie's back as she's fully curled into herself. Much to his dismay, her giggles start all over again. He takes his hand back and stares straight ahead, thinking to himself that despite Maddie's orneriness and her awkward emotions, there's no one else he wants to be with. She is the bravest girl he knows, and she has the biggest heart when it counts. Maddie loves her family, little children, and the elderly, and that's good enough for him. Mason looks over to see Maddie finally sitting upright with a very pink face. She's biting her lip so hard he's surprised it's not bleeding. At least her fit of giggling is done, and she's stopped shaking the entire church pew.

The music plays. That was quick. Everyone stands as they walk by. Chad wipes a tear from his face on his way down the aisle and Maddie whips around to bury her face in Mason's chest as her giggles start all over. Mason pats her back once more, praying they look somewhat normal as he notices a dirty look from Josie, but he figures that's fair. Mason grins at the elderly woman a few pews up who smiles at him like he's the sweetest thing for comforting a weepy Maddie. If only she really knew why Maddie will never be a bride.

They wait their turn and walk out with their row. Mason grabs a bottle of bubbles, and they head outside. Maddie reaches for his bubbles, but he holds them out of her reach as he looks down at her. "You're just going to throw them in his eyes. I'm not giving them to you."

She scowls up at him. "If I did throw them on him, then he'd have something to cry about. What a pansy."

He frowns down at her. "It's his wedding day. He's allowed to be emotional."

She crosses her arms on her chest. "If you ask me, the only one who should be crying is his wife."

He hears a gasp and turns to see Josie glaring at the two of them. Maddie whips around to face Josie. "What? Don't act like it's not true."

"Maddie. People can change you know."

She raises an eyebrow of warning at Josie. "Can they, Josie?"

Mason grabs Maddie's arm and pulls her up next to him. "Can it. Don't ruin their wedding day."

Maddie leans her head on his shoulder and looks up at him all sweet faced. "Chillax, Mason. I'm only throwing a little shade, 'cause it's awful hot out here." He hears her words, and they register but his response gets lost in the look in her eye, along with her cheek resting against his shoulder, not to mention her lips looking like they want to be kissed right about now. He shifts a little and grabs his bubbles to open them. He blows some in the air above Chad and his bride as they walk close by. Everyone hollers and whistles. Chad and his bride hop in the car with all the cans tied on the back. They drive down the street for a few blocks. Everyone chases after them for about half a block.

Maddie tugs on his arm. "Slow down, Mason. These heels are killing my feet."

Mason glances down and takes in her saucy heels along with her painted toenails, dainty ankles, and beautiful long legs from her toes to her shins. Maddie always did have long legs for being so short. "Believe me, Maddie. They're worth every bit of your pain."

Maddie knocks into him from the side. "Shut up, Mason. You try wearin' heels."

"No, thank you," he grunts out.

She throws an arm through Mason's. "Thanks for taking me as your guest to this epic wedding."

He looks down at her. "I can't tell if you're kidding or not."

She side eyes him. "Or not. There's an open bar. Take me to it."

He groans. "After your open display of idiocy, I'm not so sure you deserve a drink, but I know I do."

She elbows Mason. "Whatever, Mason. If I hadn't come with you, you'd be alone right now."

He flinches at her statement. "Well. At least there's that."

———

Maddie sips her drink and finally lets her guard down long enough to take in the reception which seems to be going pretty well, considering it's Merk the Jerk's wedding. She stands in line waiting for the bathroom when she accidentally bumps into the bride, who walks a little too close in her gorgeous flowing dress. "Oh, I'm so sorry," Maddie says as she stares at the perfectly nice, normal-looking woman, and once again wonders how she ended up with Merk the Jerk.

The bride gives her a friendly smile. "Hi. I'm sure I won't remember everyone's names, but what is your name? How do you know my husband?"

She takes a deep breath and ponders her answer. The lady sounds so genuine. She hates to burst her bubble. "Merk the.." She catches herself. "I mean, Chad and I went to school together. We were in the same class."

The bride nods her head and leans in. "Aww, then I bet you know Matty, the boy he didn't invite because he was so mean to Chad."

Maddie turns her head to lean into the wall as she chokes on her sip of rum and coke, hoping the bride will move on. She turns back. Nope, she's still there, and she looks all concerned. "Excuse me, I think I have something in my throat," she manages.

It's like the bride didn't hear her. She's so set on relaying Chad's playground tales of woe. "You wouldn't *believe* the things that boy did to my poor Chad. He bullied him on the playground, and he dragged him across the girl's bathroom by his ear. He was *just awful*."

Maddie considers the fact that this is her wedding day, and she's just as gorgeous as she can be in her white dress. Maddie hates to besmirch her dear husband's childhood memories, even though they're so far off the map they need a new zip code.

Maddie bites her tongue and debates her silence when someone bumps into her from behind.

"Oh, hey Maddie. I'm so sorry. I didn't see you there." The guy gives her a wink. "I gotta say, Mad-die, you're lookin' pretty good, and this is the *last place* I thought I'd see you."

Maddie's gaze stays on the bride. She wills Josh who is three years her senior and already been divorced two or three times to disappear. By the look on the bride's face, recognition has just struck. She blinks a few times. "You're...you're Matty."

Maddie sticks out her hand. "Yep, I'm Maddie. I'm Chad's tormentor, the playground demon from Hades." Maddie declares. "However, in my defense, I gotta tell you, your husband was better known as Merk the Jerk. It was Chad who did all the shoving of my best friend, Mason, into toilets and girl's bathrooms, but I'm betting your poor, defenseless *Chad* didn't mention any of that." Maddie gives her a wink. "I love your dress. It's absolutely gorgeous," Maddie says in all sincerity. "Your Chad is a lucky man." She clears her throat. "But you? Not so much."

The bride backs away from Maddie slowly and that's about the time Maddie realizes her voice is raised, and the room is a little too quiet. A hand rests on the small of her back. "Hey, Maddie."

Maddie takes a deep, calming breath, which only feels natural when Mason is nearby. "Mason."

The bride tears her eyes from Maddie to look Mason in the eye. "Hi, Mason," she whispers.

Mason leans in and kisses her cheek. "You are a lovely bride. Thanks so much for inviting us to your special day. We wish you all the best. We are so happy to be here, but right now, we're just going to go for some fresh air." Mason steers Maddie away from the bathroom line. Maddie walks through the small crowd with her head held high. She refuses to show any weakness. Mason leans in to whisper in her ear. "Boy, Maddie. When you step in it, you really step in it."

She wheels around to face him. By this time, they're outside. "I was actually not going to say anything, believe it or not," she says with a raised finger. "Even though she was totally painting The Jerk as a victim. I was debating letting her keep her picture-perfect idea of a helpless little boy, although he certainly was not, but then that idiot Josh bumped into me and called me by name. That's when it clicked in her brain, and I wasn't about to deny who I am when she asked me plain as day if I was Maddie the tormentor, and so I told her, and that's what you walked up on." She looks up at him. "Do you believe me?"

He laughs out loud. "Of course, I believe you. Only you could get involved in something that socially awkward."

She slumps a little to the side. "Gee, Mason, thanks for that vote of confidence."

His eyes fly to her lips. "It's that mouth of yours that gets you in trouble every time, but it's the kind of trouble I can't seem to stay away from." He reaches out and pulls her to him. "You look so beautiful in that dress." He says as he playfully snaps a spaghetti strip before trailing a finger down her arm. "Everyone saw the bride today, Maddie, but not me. I couldn't get past you." His eyes search hers.

Maddie thinks his mouth is moving but she stopped hearing. Maddie reaches for him to help him get closer to her. Their lips meet and it's just as magical as before.

Maddie looks up at her best friend, but he's so much more than that. "Mason. Are you coming home with me tonight?"

His face looks pained. "Only if we're going by a courthouse or a church on the way home."

She flinches. She feels like she just got a douse of cold water to the face. "Excuse me?"

He kisses her again, and it's as gentle as a whisper. He pulls back, but his hand still frames the side of her face. "You heard me, Maddie Dill. I'm in this with you for good, but I need to know if you feel the same way."

She pulls away from him. She can't believe how rejected she feels. "You ask too much of me."

He watches her as she steps backwards. "You ask too little of me."

MYSTERY COUPLE

THIS ICE HOUSE
IS KIND OF HOT

I met my future husband on a weekend of "chasing cleats" with my college roommate in her hometown. We went to the game to watch a bunch of semi-pro baseball players run around in their uniforms. Afterwards, we went to a local restaurant called The Ice House to hang out with the baseball team. None of the players really caught my attention, but a tall guy who seemed to be the life of the party across the room did.

When I asked about him, my friend told me I should meet him, and that he was her brother's best friend. I didn't meet him right then, but after we left the restaurant, we went to a party out in the country, and the guy ended up there too along with his brother. His brother asked me for my number, but I told him I would give it to him only if he gave it to his brother. He probably didn't like that much. He told me his brother had a girlfriend. I gave him my number anyway and went back to hanging out with the baseball players and my friend, but I watched the tall guy from afar. There was something about him that made me want to get to know him better.

After that night I didn't think any more about him because he had a girlfriend, but then a few weeks later they broke up and he called me up and asked me out. I was so excited. I told him to pick me up from work. When it came time to go on our date, I got cold feet and left work early to go home. He didn't give up when my manager told him I went home sick. He came looking for me and we spent the night sitting on the porch talking until the sun came up the next morning.

When he left to go back home, I told my roommates I was going to marry him one day. We've been married twenty-seven years and have three wonderful children. Our son ended up playing on the same semi-pro baseball team I went to watch that weekend!

- Maddie Dill
The Daily Chase

Twenty-Eight

Mason sits in his truck in the parking lot, kicking himself. *Curse me and my stupid mouth. I could have gone home with Maddie tonight. We could be on the way to her bed right now, but I had to go and ruin it by offering her forever. Why did I ever think it was a good idea to get Maddie to commit to anything? I was only half joking when I told Josie that Maddie wears running shoes. And now here I sit in the parking lot all by myself like the idiot I am, while Maddie's probably going to close the reception down. She was on her third Margarita when I walked out.* "If I wasn't afraid of her mother, I'd leave her stupid ass at the wedding dance and let her find her own way home," he mutters to himself in the rearview mirror.

Mason stares out the open window. *I should be so mad at Maddie. She messed up a perfectly good wedding by giggling during the vows. She was completely rude to the bride, and then she turned down my sort-of proposal.* He slouches down in the seat to take a miniature nap and try to get rid of the headache that's been around ever since they set foot in the church earlier, but it's not comfortable at all. He sits back up in his truck and lays his head back. "Maddie doesn't do formal very well. If we ever go to another wedding, I'll make sure it's in the middle of a cow pasture," he carries on, chuckling to himself.

He's just about to fall asleep when he hears someone puking

outside. He jumps out of the truck when he spies Maddie's long red hair. He runs over to hold back her hair and turns her away just before she goes to puke down the side of his truck bed. He whips out his hankie he keeps for special occasions and hands it to her. "Wipe your face."

She turns toward him. She's so drunk he doesn't know how she's still standing. He wipes her face again with the handkerchief. He's none too gentle, as he's still peeved at her. She starts to fall sideways into his side mirror. He grabs hold of her and pulls her toward him. She wraps her arms around him and buries her face in his chest. "Oh, Mason. What would I do without you?" She looks up at him. "I do love you, you know." Her eyes close and she promptly passes out. He somehow wrestles her into his truck and helps her with her seatbelt.

He rushes around and gets in on his side and tries not to think about the words Maddie said; the words he's been waiting to hear from her for so long. His mind races as he drives down the highway. He wonders if she meant it. Her hot little hand rests on his thigh, but then it starts traveling. He grabs a hold of it and lays it back on the seat.

"But I like your junk," she slurs out of her loose, drunk lips before she starts at it again. He grabs a hold of her hand and keeps it in place on the seat. Soon enough, she's snoring.

He releases her limp hand. He sighs. "Maddie Dill. You are a real treat," he mumbles as he glances down at her sleeping form. "I doubt you'll remember any of this tomorrow."

Mason is worn out and then some by the time he gets back to Maddie's house. He taps her on the face. She doesn't stir. He leans over and blows in her ear. She swats at the air. He squeezes her shoulder with his hand. "Maddie. Wake up."

She rolls on to her back and curls into his seat before she starts snoring again. He gives up. He cracks his window and lays his head back on the seat. "I guess I'm sleeping over with Maddie after all," he mutters.

———

Morning comes a little too bright and a little too early. Maddie's staring at him.

"Want to come in and make some more pickles and fries?"

He raises an eyebrow. "At 6:30 a.m.? Don't you have more journalism articles to write?"

"Nope. It's a flexible position. As long as I meet my deadlines, they don't care what hours I work." She looks at him again. "So, no dill pickles and French fries?"

Mason really doesn't want to. He's exhausted from trying to sleep sitting up in the truck last night. He's got a crick in his neck. Maddie telling him she loved him last night really threw him for a loop. What Mason really wants is space, but her voice sounds so hopeful.

"Sure." He hops out of the truck and follows her inside. She goes over to the coffeepot and starts it up. He sits down at the kitchen table and waits. Done setting up the coffeepot, she plops down in a chair across from him and traces shapes on the table. "Last night was interesting, huh?"

He bites his lip. "Which part? The part where you laughed at the groom, told the bride how awful her new husband is, or the part where you basically threw up all down the side of my truck?"

Her eyebrows shoot up. She looks down at her wrinkled dress. "Well, I missed puking on my dress, anyways."

He searches her face for any tell-tale signs of her remembering professing her love for him. He doesn't see any, but she is as stubborn as a mule, so he's not that surprised that the only time she tells him how she really feels is when she's falling-down drunk, but it still stings.

The coffeepot goes off. He hops up and grabs two cups, pours her a cup of black coffee and hands it to her. He pours half a cup for himself and fills the rest of it with milk before he sits back down. He takes a sip. "You really up for making dill pickles and fries?"

She takes a sip of coffee and wrinkles her nose. "Nope." She gives him a funny look. "What I really want is a nap. You want to take a nap?"

He's not sure how to answer. "Okay."

She stands up and reaches for his hand. "Come on. Let's go." He walks behind Maddie all the way up the stairs. He follows her down the hallway to her room and steps through the door behind her. He walks over to her window and looks out the pane he knows so well from the other side. He peers down into the yard to where his truck sits in her driveway. He looks over at Maddie and wishes like so many times before that she was his. She flops down the edge of her bed. Her black chiffon pokes out from beneath her deep purple satiny dress. He's shocked to see the pink, flowery quilted bedspread that she sits on as her legs dangle over the edge of her bed. It's so feminine and so unlike the rest of her.

Maddie looks up at him. Her slumberous gaze is like a siren's call, just like her bed-head red hair that sticks up every which way as a few stray hairs fall over her lost, dark eyes. Mason can't help but smile at the little bit of leftover girl she used to be peeks out at him. He pretends to look at his phone as he snaps a picture. He feels bad about it, but not bad enough. He knows it's pathetic to keep a picture as proof of her desire for him, but he can't help himself. He shoves his phone in his pocket.

He sits down beside her. "Scoot your butt over. I'm laying down."

He lays with his back to her. After being rejected last night, he vows not to chase after her anymore. She sneaks up and curls into his back. Her arm comes around his waist. She digs her chin into his back just enough to cause him discomfort.

"I know I'm hard to love, Mason," she whispers as her hand reaches up to rest on his chest. "Thanks for loving me, anyways."

———

Maddie wakes with a start. She flinches under the steady gaze of her mother who stands in the doorframe. She tries to remove her hand from Mason's, but he holds tight. Her mom shakes her head. "Oh, Maddie. If I had more nerve, I'd send a photo to his mom right now. Talk about a head explodin' and rollin' out the door."

"Thanks for that visual, Mrs. Dill. I just as soon my mom keeps her head," Mason growls. His eyes remain closed.

Maddie snuggles into him and closes her eyes. Her mom claps her hands. "Lord above, we have a weddin' to plan," she exclaims like a deranged Southern bell.

Maddie's eyes fly open again. She stares at her mother in horror. Her mother makes a face of surprise at Maddie before she scurries down the hall.

Maddie flops back on her pillow. "That was so not funny."

Mason lets go of her hand. He moves over onto his back and stares up at the ceiling. "I'm not laughin'."

She scoots over to lay her head on his arm. "I know."

He turns his head a little sideways. She doesn't like the look in his eye. "Maddie."

"Yeah."

"I'd be on board with a wedding."

Ugh. Not this again. She rolls her eyes. "Stop it, Mason. You're like a broken record."

He sits up and puts on his shoes. "Maybe I only know one song." He stands up and goes to stand by her window. He leans against the wall by the edge of the pane. "You know how many times I stood down there and looked up here, wonderin' what you were doing, or if you were thinkin' about me?"

Her whole face flushes. "No."

He looks over at her. "Plenty, Maddie. I can't count how many nights I stared up at your window, wonderin' if you were ever going to forgive me for fallin' for you." His eyes water. He looks like the insecure high-school boy she used to know, and she hates herself for it. "But you never did, Maddie. You just let me go." He bites his thumbnail. "And now I'm lettin' you go." His eyes turn a little hard. It's a face she's never seen on Mason, and she doesn't like it. "I know you love me, Maddie. You told me so," he states.

She stands up and moves toward him. "Mason, I..."

"Don't. Don't say another word," he cuts her off. "Just stay away from me. I can't be your friend anymore."

Maddie feels like the floor just dropped out beneath her and she can't find her feet. "What about the dill pickle contest?"

He stares her down. "I forfeit." He walks clear around her and out the door. She goes to her window and watches him back out of her drive. She sits down on her bed once more.

What just happened? It's like my life is stuck on reruns. Mason and I were friends again, and it was wonderful. But then he wanted more, and just like before I refused him. "This time I'm the one who's hurting. It's my heart that's breaking," she whispers through her tears.

There's a knock at her bedroom door. She looks up, hoping to see Mason, but it's her mom. "Maddie Dill, what kind of mess did you get yourself into this time?"

Maddie wipes a tear from her face. "The Mason French kind."

Her mom sits beside Maddie on the bed and holds her tight. "You and Mason have another tiff?"

Maddie nods her head. "Yeah."

She squeezes Maddie even tighter. "You want to talk about it?"

"No," Maddie wails as she shoves her face into her mom's shoulder. "Why can't I be happy being a small-town housewife, Mom?"

Her mom throws her head back and laughs. "Oh, Maddie-girl. You're twenty-three. You don't have to know everything right now."

Maddie breathes out. "That's good because I don't."

Her mom leans away from Maddie just enough to look her in the face. "Do you know who you love?"

She rolls her eyes. "It's complicated, Mom."

Her mother snorts. "No, Maddie, it's not. You either love him or you don't. Everything else will work itself out. You'll see."

She drops her head. "It doesn't matter what I feel. He's gone for good. I've ruined everything."

Her mom squeezes her knee. "Nonsense, Maddie. He's a man. Just be patient. Men are impulsive. They want things when they want them. Sometimes it takes them a while to come around to an idea and sometimes they don't know what they want." Her mom winks at Maddie. "It's up to us women to show them."

Maddie frowns. "That sounds like a riddle with no answer."

Her mother smiles at her. "Maddie, if you love Mason then you need to tell him, preferably when you're not three sheets to the wind. You'd be surprised by how much more it might mean to him." Her mom squeezes her knee again, hard enough it hurts a little bit. "And Maddie, you don't need liquid courage to face your feelings for him. I raised you better than that." She walks out of her daughter's room.

Maddie stares down at her hands. "Great. I'm being so difficult no one can love me today," she says before she promptly bursts into tears all over again, something she never used to do before Mason French walked back into her life.

Twenty-Nine

Mason drives down the road, muttering to himself once more. "What is it about Maddie that makes me give out ultimatums? What am I, stupid? No, I'm not stupid. A guy has his pride." He slaps his steering wheel. "If I don't have that what do I have? Not Maddie Dill, that's for sure. She belongs to no one. She's like an island. An island I want to live on forever. This is so annoying."

He is a little surprised to find himself parked outside his grandpa's home, but it's like something flipped inside once he told Maddie off. He thinks he's found his backbone. Mason marches through the front door and into his front room. "Grandpa. I've got something to say."

His grandpa looks up at Mason from behind his newspaper. His old blue eyes twinkle. "Well, then. Go on and say it, boy." Mason almost loses his nerve, but being called a boy drives the last nail in the coffin.

He takes a deep breath. "Grandpa, I don't like saying this, and I wish I felt different about it, but I don't want to buy you out."

A smile breaks out on his grandpa's face. Mason can't believe it. "Who is she, son?" his grandpa asks.

"What," is the only word Mason can get out.

"Who's the lucky girl who's got a hold of you? I assume this is the reason you aren't settling down with my store." His grandpa chuckles at his own joke.

"Um, there's no girl, Grandpa," Mason grumbles.

His grandpa looks a little confused. "Is there a guy?"

Mason shakes his head. "No, no, there's no guy."

His grandpa leans back in his chair. "What's left?"

Mason tries to make him understand. "It's just. I have dreams, Grandpa. I want to travel, and I can't do that if I'm tied to a business."

His grandpa nods his head. "This is true. What job are you going to have so you can travel?" Mason can't believe his grandpa is being so calm.

He thinks hard. "Welding. I'm going to be a traveling welder who takes jobs on contract."

His grandpa scratches his chin. "Mm-hmm. I didn't know that was a thing."

Mason nods his head again. "Oh, yeah. There's lots of jobs like that for young single people who are unattached and without a family." Mason says with a smile. "This way I can see the world and I'll also be working."

His grandpa studies him. "Well, that all sounds real nice." He rocks back and forth in his chair. "Say, whatever happened to that spitfire, Maddie Dill? She seemed like the real deal. She had what I call grit."

Mason sticks a hand in his back pocket. "Yeah, she has grit alright." Mason frowns down at his grandpa. "I thought you didn't like her."

His grandpa chuckles. "I never said I didn't like her."

Mason sits down in a chair. "Well, I just figured so, since her mom stole my mom's fiancée, you know."

His grandpa laughs out loud. "Yeah, I know." He leans forward and talks quietly. "But I figure the Lord works in mysterious ways, son, and your parents were meant to be together, otherwise they wouldn't be." He raises his eyebrows and claps his hands together. "All I'm thinking is, you marry a girl like Maddie Dill, and you'll never be bored. That's for dang sure."

Mason's grandma pops her head around the corner. "Steve, you stop your talking about that girl." She looks over at Mason and points at his grandpa. "Your grandpa has had his eye on making that girl his grand-daughter since she was six years old and shoved Chad's face in the mud right in front of his mother for calling you a four-eyed sissy. I swear I heard about that red-headed firecracker for weeks."

Mason can't help but smile at the memory. It was an awesome moment. He shakes his head. "You're both right. Maddie was my fierce defender." His eyes dim a little bit and he clears his throat. "But not anymore. She'll probably go right back to forgetting me like she did the last time."

Mason heads for the kitchen. "Hey, Grandma, you want to teach me how to make fried pickles?"

His grandma grins at him. "Are you entering the contest, then?"

Mason coughs. "I suppose. Maddie kind of promised the senior center we would, but I'm having a heck of a time with my pickles. They taste like cardboard crap." He clears his throat. "We made some together and they turned out pretty good, but when we make them by ourselves, that's when we both have problems."

His grandma scoffs. "That's probably just a coincidence. With my help, you'll figure out these pickles. No food ever got the best of me," she promises.

Mason tries not to sigh as his grandma launches into a spiel about what order to go in to make the best pickle, and how to dip it in the oil just right and the batter just right, and then you heat the oil just right...

Mason does his level best to take her advice. Soon enough, he's dippin' and fryin' those pickles, and they're not half bad. He thinks he might give mean Maddie a run for her money after all.

Thirty

M addie can't believe it's been a whole week and she hasn't heard a word from Mason. She's been out to the pond more times than she'd like to admit, but he's not there. He's avoiding her plain and simple, and she can't believe how much it hurts. "Ah, well. It'll give me time to work on my articles anyways," she grumbles as she steps inside the newspaper office.

Jim gives her a funny look and that's when she remembers her promise to him to interview all the local businesses to run a little personal story on their beginnings, and what they meant to her as a kid growing up in our small town. She grabs her notebook and her laptop and pops back out. "Well, this will be a great way to fill up a Friday. I bet I can get one side of the street, anyways," she comments. Maddie gets a funny look from her best friend's mom, and that's when she realizes she's talking to herself out loud again.

Maddie clamps her mouth shut and hurries into the western store down on the corner. Shannon gives her a funny look when she steps inside. Maddie stops for a second. Come to think of it, so has every person she's seen this morning. *What's that about* she wonders for a few seconds before she shrugs it off. Mason always told her she thinks too highly of herself. Maybe he's right. They can't all be looking at her.

Maddie visits with Shannon a little about how her mom and her mom's best friend took over the business twenty years ago, and how they've changed a little of the inventory with the times. It goes pretty smoothly except for Shannon staring at Maddie intensely like she's waiting for Maddie to do something strange. Shannon's staring at her is a little more than awkward, but Maddie's got local interviews to do for Joe and she's determined to get them done. If there's one thing she doesn't want on her letter of recommendation, it's being a slacker and not meeting deadlines.

Shannon lights up when she talks about the big rodeo their little town has once a year and how it's been so good for business. "My favorite room in this whole store is the boot room, because I like to play a little game with myself. Whenever I see a person walk in that room, I try to guess which boots they would pick out. I have to say I've gotten pretty good at it over the years," Shannon says with a smile. "I've spent a lot of time in my mom's store over the years." Her eyes shine bright. "Now that she's gone it's my store, and I'm determined to make her proud."

Maddie can't help it. Her heart pinches a little at Shannon's words. What a sweet legacy to carry on. The boot room catches Maddie's eye. It's been so long since she bought the one pair of boots she still owns. Maddie steps inside the boot room and wanders through them. They're all so gorgeous with their bright colors and intricate designs. It's a hard choice. She sees a few that are beautiful, but she's not sure they're her. But then Maddie spies a rather plain-looking pair up in the corner. They look more vintage with their worn appearance and square toe. Maddie thinks they're not much to look at, but she knows before she puts them on, they're the ones. Maddie plops down on the bench and tugs one over her foot. It's ridiculous, but there's something about them that makes her feel like home. And then there's Mason, who stands in the doorway of the small room. "Shannon," he says.

Shannon's head jerks up along with Maddie's at the sound of his voice. "Oh, hey, Mason."

He clears his throat and doesn't give Maddie so much as a passing glance. "So, I was just stopping by to see if we're still on for tonight."

Maddie opens her mouth to say something, but nothing comes out.

Shannon blushes. "Yeah, sure. You can just stop by the store at seven to pick me up."

Maddie grips the boot tight, so she doesn't chuck it at Mason's head. She knows one thing; she's not buying anything in this stupid store. Maddie shoves her feet in her shoes and marches past Shannon. Maddie bumps into Mason a little too hard as she walks by. He moves out of her way and goes right back to talking to Shannon. Maddie grabs up her laptop and notebook and hits the door, making it fly open.

"The sooner I leave this one-horse town the better," Maddie mutters as she heads down the sidewalk.

Maddie breezes right past the furniture store without even realizing it. She does an about face and marches inside to visit with the owner, a master craftsman. Maddie takes down notes of their interview and tries to focus, but it's so hard. She can't believe Mason's taking Shannon out, or that it's got her all tied up in knots, which is exactly what Mason wants. He's just doing it to make her jealous. She can't believe how well it's working. Rick clears his throat. Maddie looks up from her writing pad. "I'm so sorry, Rick. Were you saying something?"

Rick smiles his little smile. "I can see someone's on your mind."

Maddie looks around his store and tries to keep the tears out of her eyes. She's losing it. "Yeah."

Rick pats her hand. "It'll be alright. Love can hit when you least expect it."

Maddie clears her throat. "I wouldn't go that far."

He chuckles. "You're one of the hard-headed ones, huh."

Maddie frowns. "I'm not hard-headed. I'm just…" She sighs. "I don't know what I am."

Rick slaps a flyer down in front of her. "You're being challenged. That's what you are."

Maddie picks it up. She can hardly believe what she sees as she stares into her drunk face beneath her messy bedhead hair sticking up everywhere like a siren as she sits in her satin dress looking up at the camera with eyes full of want. This horrific image of her is splashed all over the flyer that's a Wanted Poster. Her eyes can hardly believe what they're reading. "Wanted, the Worst Pickle Fryer in Town. We Duel at Dawn on Saturday—in the Town Square. The Frenches Own the Best Fried Pickle Claim to Fame. Make It Count, Maddie Dill. Mason French." There's a picture of Mason standing over a frying pan with his charming smile. Maddie snatches up the flyer and turns back to a silent Rick. Her hands shake with anger. "Where did you get this?"

Rick's as serious as can be. "Where do you think I got it? Mason brought it in here." Rick's knowing smile is back, but Maddie can barely see through her rage. "If I didn't know better, I'd say he's tryin' to get your attention."

Maddie stands up and about knocks the bar stool over she was sitting on. "He's got my attention alright, and a few other things."

Maddie stomps outside and just about runs Mason over on the sidewalk. She frowns up at him and slaps the flyer against his chest. "Really, Mason? You're going to these lengths just to talk to me?"

Mason covers her hand with his and squeezes it tighter than she thought he would. "No, Maddie. I'm trying to shut you up." Mason stares her down. "I've put up with your ridiculous grievances and accusations against my family long enough. I'm challenging you to a cook-off in front of the entire town. I'm bringing out the propane grill and we're cooking over the flame. After Saturday, they'll be no reason for you or me to speak to each other ever again."

Maddie rips her hand from his. The flyer falls to the ground between them. "Fine," she says before she wheels around and stomps off.

"Litterbug," Mason hollers after her.

She holds her head high and keeps on walking.

"Maddie." She turns to see Rick's head peeking out the door. "You forgot your laptop and your notebook."

Maddie starts toward a worried Rick and a smirking Mason. *So much for a dramatic exit.*

Thirty-One

Shannon and Mason sit outside in the back of his truck at the pond. "I'm sure glad I brought my lawn chairs. They're a lot more comfortable than sitting on the truck bed." Shannon scoots closer to him. "What're you doin'," he asks.

She taps his hand. "Relax, Mason. I ain't makin' a move on you. I'm practically an engaged woman. I'm just makin' sure it looks like something's going on in case anyone shows up lookin' for you."

Mason sighs. "Yeah, right. Like Maddie Dill would come out here lookin' for me. She wouldn't even look at me at the store today."

Shannon shoulder bumps him. "That's because she's hurtin', Mason. Trust me, I know the feeling. It about broke my heart when Ryan stopped talkin' to me and I thought we were through." Shannon laughs. "I still joke if my fourth cousin hadn't come to town and Ryan hadn't seen us out at the movies and thought we were on a date, he never would have come back to me."

Mason shakes his head. "Why do some people have to realize what they're losing before they come to their senses?"

She laughs. "I guess it's the same reason we all take things and people for granted on some level, Mason."

Mason glances up at the stars. "It sure is nice out tonight."

Shannon nods. "Yep. I bet Ryan's sleeping under the stars tonight. He loves driving cattle."

Mason slaps his hands on his knees. "He can have it. That kind of life's not for me. I like to sleep indoors."

Shannon looks over at him. "What do you enjoy?"

Mason fidgets. "Bringing things together."

"That makes sense."

He nods. "Yep. It's amazing what fire, heat, and high temperatures can do."

Shannon looks a little ornery when she looks at him again. "Have you tried that with Maddie?"

Mason blushes. "I can't believe you said that."

Shannon giggles. "It's just a suggestion." She looks up at him. "She really wanted those boots today. I could tell."

Mason rolls his eyes. "Well, maybe if she didn't throw such hissy fits she would have them right now."

Shannon laughs out loud. "Now you sound just like her."

Mason stares out at the moonlight on the water. "Yeah."

They sit in silence for a little while. Mason thinks he hears a twig snap from somewhere in the darkness. Shannon grabs his face and pulls it to hers. They share a kiss and it's nice, but it's nowhere near what Mason feels when Maddie's lips are on his. Shannon stops kissing him, but she holds her forehead against his.

"What are you doing?" he whispers.

She smiles at him. "Faking it," she whispers back before leaning her head on his shoulder while they gaze at the moon. Mason wants to look back so badly toward the noise that grows quieter and quieter, but he doesn't dare give away their game. He almost feels bad that Maddie might have seen them kissing but he just can't. After all, Maddie's the one who rejected him more times than he'd like to remember. He looks out at the pond.

"I can't believe it was just the other night that Maddie and I were out here, having so much fun enjoying each other's company, and now she won't even talk to me," he whispers.

Shannon holds his hand. "She'll come back to you, Mason. I really think she will."

Mason shakes his head. "I shouldn't have gone with my impulses and made that flyer, but I meant every word I said. Besides, I stand a better chance at winning the contest if Maddie is good and pissed off. She's never backed down from a challenge and she's not about to start now."

Shannon giggles. "Are you sure this is about a contest, Mason, or is it about Maddie?"

Mason leans back in his lawn chair. "At this point, I have no idea." He stares across the pond. "All I know is I'll bring her to her knees one way or another."

Thirty-Two

Maddie groans as she stands at the stove, burning another batch of dill pickles just like she did the day before and the day before that.

She FaceTimes Alex. "I'm so pathetic. I can't concentrate long enough to do a decent job on any of them. I just keep seeing Shannon and Mason sitting in the back of his truck at *our pond*, kissing and gazing up at the moon, like that's not our special place, and our special thing. It's like the *Déjà Vu* song by Olivia Rodrigo that I used to find so funny, but not anymore. I know exactly how she feels."

Alex groans. "It's frigging 6:00 a.m., Maddie. I need my sleep." Alex ends their FaceTime call.

Maddie stands in front of the stove, staring at her big old fried pickle mess. Tears run down her face, and she can't make them stop.

Her mom steps into the room and Maddie's dam bursts. She plops down in her chair. "What the hell is going on with me? I never cry. I didn't cry when my favorite horse died, or when Grandpa fell down and broke his hip when I was ten and I had to saddle up the horse and take off for the house. I didn't even cry when everyone in town was bawling their eyes out over the town's prized sow that somehow disappeared into the woods down by the river for three days."

197

Her mom claps a hand over her mouth, but her laughter sneaks out. "A pig, Maddie? Really?"

Maddie throws up her hands. "Everyone else was crying, but I couldn't, no matter how hard I tried. Okay? You don't remember that darn pig that ran off a week before the town's Bacon-Fest?" Maddie slaps the table at the same time she laugh/cries. "It was like she knew she had an execution date down at Barnett's Farm. She was the biggest sow they'd ever had. Her size even made the county newspaper. And then she made the paper again after her crazy disappearance." Maddie wipes her tears away and laughs a little. "That sow had Trevor running in circles trying to find her."

Her mom stares at Maddie who might be having some sort of breakdown. "What happened to the sow, honey? Did they find her?"

Maddie giggles through her tears. "Of course they did, and wouldn't you know it? It was Mason who found her; the one boy in town who was terrified of pigs and any large animal that looked like it could squash him flat. He came running out of the woods hollering and yelling, with that stupid sow right behind him squealing all the way. Mason ran all the way up to our yard and climbed up my tree." Maddie's laughing so hard she can hardly finish her story. "That stupid sow sat at the base of the tree squealing and snorting until dad came out and corralled her into a trailer to haul her to town." Maddie shakes her head back and forth. "It took me an hour to get Mason out of that tree. He was shaking so bad. That was quite a day. I'd never seen a pig tree a boy before. I guess that's why I couldn't quit laughing, but Mason sure didn't find it funny."

The smoke detector goes off. Maddie jumps up from the table. "Darn it." She whips open the stove and goes to grab the fry pan but stops just before she touches it bare-handed. She whips on an oven mitt and pulls out her potato wedges that are burnt all to heck. Maddie drops the pan on the stove. "I'm not doing any better with the fries than the pickles. I'll never win the contest." Maddie throws her head back and growls as the smoke detector keeps beeping piercing her ears.

"Maddie, turn that darn thing off," her mom hollers.

Maddie plops back down in her chair. "I can't reach it, mom. The ceiling's too high."

Her mom rushes across the room and whips out a kitchen chair to stand on as she disassembles the smoke detector. "All you have to do is take out the batteries. Is that so hard to understand?"

Maddie coughs. "Speaking of things that are hard to understand, did I tell you Mason went on a date with Shannon?" Maddie spits out her name.

Her mom raises an eyebrow. "You may have mentioned it once or twice in the last hour and a half, yes." Her mom turns off the oven. "What's going on?"

Maddie takes the wadded-up flyer from her pocket and lays it on the table. Her mom unwrinkles it and flattens it out. She studies the picture of Maddie that Mason snapped the morning after the wedding, the one that makes her look very wanton. Maddie can't believe he would humiliate her like this just like she can't believe she's not running out of town at this exact moment, given everyone in town has seen her like that. Her mom giggles a little and then a lot, and then she can't stop. Maddie thinks she might pee herself.

"Thanks for your sympathy and kindness. I hope you're wearing Depends," she states.

Her mom's giggling turns into raucous laughter. "My Maddie," she announces. You are a treat."

Maddie rolls her eyes. "Well, everyone's going to know what kind of treat I can be after the contest on Saturday. My pickles taste like crap and the wedges are all burnt." Maddie taps the table. "I can't think straight, Mom. What is going on?"

Her mom reaches out and squeezes Maddie's hand. "You're falling in love."

Maddie shakes her head. "I can't be in love. I've been around Mason for less than a month. That's just crazy."

Her mom studies her. "Is it? You've been writing all these meet-cutes, but have you been paying any sort of attention to them? I've read them all. It seems to me when you know, you know." Her mom squeezes Maddie's shoulder. "Guys like Mason don't come along every day."

She stares at the mess on the stove. "I can't be in love with Mason. He's such a wimp. He's emotional. He's like a girl." Except for his kisses. There's nothing girly about those hot lips of his, lips that were just on Shannon's down by the pond. Maddie grabs the flyer and rips it in half. She doesn't want any part of Mason French touching her now that he's kissed another girl. "What am I going to do?"

"Maddie, girl. You're old enough to know your own mind. I'm not making decisions for you especially when it comes to love. Just remember, love is patient, love is kind. Love is not self-seeking, it keeps no record of wrong. Love is loyalty and devotion." Her mom looks a little too satisfied. "I know someone who embodies all these character traits and if you're honest with yourself, you do, too."

Maddie slaps the kitchen table. "Stop saying I'm in love. You don't know anything," she yells.

Her mom raises her hands in the air. "Alright, Maddie. Alright. I thought you wanted my help, but if you're going to yell at me, you're on your own." Her mom leans in and taps Maddie's chin. "Just remember which one of us got our man." Maddie frowns again.

"You're so annoying," she says to her mom's ever-present secretive smile.

Her mom hops up and swings her hips back and forth so wide she almost hits the wall before turning back to wink. "I did, Maddie. I got my man," she says all saucy like an old-time actress out of a black-and-white movie.

Maddie sits at the table and thinks about her mom's story. She said she just told him how she felt. "I should be able to tell him how I feel, but do I want to? What do I want to happen? He's going to be here, in this little town, forever. Can I give up my dreams of being a big-city journalist for him?" she whispers to herself as leans against the kitchen wall. Maddie goes through the pictures in her phone. Mason smiles back at her with his sincere gaze and secret smile that's just for her. Her chest hurts. She wonders for the first time if she can live without him.

She goes to the stove and tosses all the burnt pickles and fries in the trash and sets the pan outside the backdoor with a huge sigh. "I'm definitely going to disgrace my family in the duel on Saturday, but I can't back out. If I forfeit, I'm not a Dill," she vows.

Thirty-Three

Mason wakes from a dead sleep. He glances at the clock. It's 4:00 a.m., and he's regretting the stupid contest. He has been since the day Maddie slapped him on the chest with the flyer, but his stupid pride won't let him out of it now. He packs up all his cooking supplies in the truck before heading upstairs to shower before going down to the town square.

———

Maddie sits on the bed of her dad's truck in her overalls, wearing her favorite flannel shirt beneath. Mason thinks she's every farm boy's dream in her adorable outfit, clear down to her favorite flowery boots. Her red hair is pulled back in a swishy ponytail. Her brown eyes stare at him. He stares right back. Silence sits between them. It's him who looks away first. He heads for the stage to set up his work station.

She saunters up the stairs to the stage that had been set up for the event with her tub full of cooking supplies. "Mason."

He turns to face her. "Maddie."

She clears her throat. "Did you have a nice date with Shannon?"

He smiles down at her. "Yep."

She smiles even bigger at him. "Does her boyfriend know you were kissin' her out at the pond?"

His face falls. He's so busted. "Wouldn't you like to know?"

She wrinkles her nose. "I do know. I didn't think you were the type to be kissin' other people's girlfriends."

He shrugs. "How do you know any of this happened, Maddie Dill, unless you were following me around, spying on me?" He gives her a wink. "If I didn't know better, I'd say you still care."

Her self-assured grin falters a little. "Whatever. Let's just get this over with."

Miguel, the town Mayor, stands off to the side. "Welcome one and all and thank you for coming to our taste test to settle the Dill Pickle war between the Frenches and the Dills. In less than a minute, the contest will begin. These two will have one hour to make the perfect French fry and fried dill pickle." He waves a hand to the crowd. "You all will be the Judges." Mason stands beside Maddie who scowls up at him. He fights back a grin. Maddie's definitely ticked. If she's mad about him kissing Shannon, then that means she still cares. He leans down to say something in Maddie's ear. A sound like a tornado siren goes off. "Fryers, you may fry," Miguel calls out.

Mason turns away from Maddie and starts mixing his spices. As many times as he's done it this summer, he doesn't have to think. He dredges his pickles and goes to throw them in his frying pan but hesitates when he sees the oil isn't popping. Mason picks the pan up to check the heat. The flame is gone. He glances at Maddie who's looking all intent at her station, but he isn't fooled. He knows she turned off his flame. Mason turns his flame back on and waits for the oil to heat up. Maddie leans over to grab something from her tub. Mason drops a handful of salt in her mixing bowl. He hears laughter behind them. He keeps on working.

Eventually Mason gets a batch of pickles made, with no help from Maddie who keeps messing with his flame every time he turns around. Mason keeps busy dropping cayenne pepper in Maddie's frying oil and stealing a supply or two from her every chance he gets. It helps that his arms are longer than hers.

By the time half an hour has gone by, neither of them has gotten much of their own cooking done. Mason grabs Maddie's arm and yanks her to him to whisper in her ear. "If we keep this up neither of us will get our fries done."

Maddie sticks out her hand surprising him. "I call a truce. Let's make the wedges together. It's not fair to the people."

Mason has his doubts, but they shake on it. "Okay then."

Mason takes his bowl and her bowl and combines them. Maddie turns on the oven and prepares the pan. Together, they coat and season 100 potato wedges crammed into two pans in record time. They open the oven doors and stick them in. Mason cleans up his station and Maddie cleans up hers. She holds a pickle out to him to taste. He takes a bite and just about gags. Mason coughs, chokes, and sputters on the pepper that burns like fire. Maddie reaches over and snags one of his. She wrinkles her little turned-up nose at him. "It's a little undercooked and a whole lot of sour."

Mason grabs the giant Ranch bottle from Maddie's tub. "Maybe it's better with Ranch?" He makes a small puddle of it on a plate. They dip the pickles in and take one more bite. Maddie smiles up at him. "It's definitely better."

Mason opens his oven and takes out the potato wedges. Maddie looks confused. "The oven didn't beep."

He nods. "I know but it just felt right." Mason studies Maddie. "You know what I mean?"

Maddie smiles really big at him. "Yeah. I know exactly what you mean." She removes the other pan of wedges from her side, turns off the oven, and lays the pan on the stove top. "Set that pan down right now, French Fry."

Mason doesn't know what Maddie's gettin' at, but her tone has his attention. He sets the pan back down on the stove top. Maddie turns off his oven and pulls Mason in for the hottest kiss of his life. Sometime later, Maddie lets go of him. She turns to the crowd as she takes his hand and leans into the microphone. "Y'all can come up here for your French fries, I've already got mine."

Mason nudges Maddie out of the way and leans down in the mic. "And I've got my Dill Pickle." Maddie walks off stage and he's right behind her. They walk down the steps and run right into their parents. The look on Mason's mom's face throws him right back to his elementary school days when she forbade him time and time again to stop running around with Maddie Dill. It didn't work then, and it won't work now. "Mom," he warns.

"Mason. I'd like to have a talk in private please," she insists in a voice as stiff as peanut brittle.

Mason squeezes Maddie's hand. He doesn't dare look at Maddie. She's probably about to crack up. She always found his mother's anger a little too amusing. "Whatever you say can be said right here, Mother."

His mother stares at him harder. "I don't want you taking up with *that girl*."

Maddie snorts.

I pray she can keep her mouth shut this one time, he thinks.

"What's so wrong with me?" Maddie says as she steps between Mason and his mother.

His mother stares at Mason like she'd like to burn a hole clean through his forehead. "You know how I feel about her," her voice grows more shrill by the second.

Maddie steps closer to Mason's mother. She waves her hand in the air to break his mom's stare. "I'm with Mason now, Mrs. French. You're just going to have to accept it."

Mason's mom's face turns beet red. Her mouth drops open and then it shuts again. Her eyes fall on Maddie's face, and they harden. "You're just as deceitful as your mother. You are not welcome in my home," she declares.

Maddie straightens her shoulders. "Don't worry about that. I've never been in your home, Mrs. French. I don't go where I'm not welcome." Maddie takes a deep breath. "But Mason has been in our home plenty of times. He's always welcome there."

Maddie's mom clears her throat. "That's right, Mason. We love having you over."

Mason's mother turns on Mrs. Dill. "I'll just bet you do. You probably all sit around and laugh over what kind of fit I'd be having if I only knew he was there, enjoying your company."

"Kind of like the fit you're throwing now," Maddie's mom mutters.

Mason's mom's eyes go wide. She looks at Maddie's mom like she could kill her right in front of everyone. "It's not enough that you stole my fiancée, now you want to steal my son?" She turns to Mason's dad. "Say something."

Mason's dad gives his wife a pleading look mixed with sadness before he turns back to Maddie. "Welcome to the family, Maddie."

Mason's mother stomps her foot. "It figures you would betray me like this. I can't believe this is happening to me."

Maddie's mom steps closer to Mason's mother, who looks like she might spontaneously combust at any minute. "What happened between us has nothing to do with them. I'm sorry I hurt your feelings. I never meant for that to happen, but as you can see, you can't always choose who you fall in love with. Sometimes it just happens. Maddie and Mason aren't trying to hurt anyone. They're only trying to be happy. Maddie is my daughter. I'm here to support her and that's what I'm going to do."

Maddie's mom lays a hand on Mason's arm. "And Mason will always be your son. I wouldn't have it any other way, but I'm awfully proud to call him son-in-law." Maddie's mom moves to stand beside Mason. She looks his mom in the face. "It would mean a lot to Maddie and Mason if we could put our differences aside for their sakes, if not for ours. It's not healthy to be so bitter."

No one says anything as they stare at the two women.

Mason's mom turns to his dad. "I'd like to go home now."

They walk away, but Mason's dad turns back to look at him. "I'll see you at home, son." He waves at Mason who waves back.

Maddie's mom turns to look at Mason. She lets out a big breath. "Well. That went better than expected. We're all still in one piece, anyways." She hugs Maddie and Mason together. "We're going to take off, too. I'll see ya when I see ya. We love you guys."

Maddie turns to look up at Mason. "I'm sorry if I was too short with your mom, but we're not kids, anymore, Mason. You're going to have to stand up for yourself."

Mason smiles down at her. "I suppose, but you did a fantastic job standing up for me. I didn't mind."

Maddie rolls her eyes. "It's just like old times on the playground."

He leans in and kisses her soundly. "Not entirely, Maddie. I get the perks of having a gorgeous best friend who's also my girlfriend."

Thirty~Four

Maddie breathes a little easier now that it's just the two of them as they hang back while everyone tries their pickles and fries. Mason still has a hold of her hand. "Did you mean it, Maddie? Am I really yours?"

She leans into him. "I do. I only want to be with you."

He wipes a tear from his eye. "That's good, because I'm not buying out my grandpa."

Her head's so full of feelings she can only hear herself as she talks out loud. "I've thought about it a lot these past few days. Even though I want to be a city girl, I want to be with you more. Being local isn't ideal, but I'd stay for you."

He coughs. "Maddie. I said I'm not staying here."

Her ears perk up. "You're not?"

He grins full out. "No. I'm going to be a traveling welder, so I can follow you wherever you go."

She can't stop smiling as she looks up at him. "Maybe you could make our resume, you know, like a wanted poster for a traveling welder and a journalist." She gives him a wink. "It certainly drew a crowd today."

He laughs out loud. "Yeah, I think they were all waiting for World War three to break out, though. They're probably more than a little disappointed we didn't have a knock-down, drag-out fight up on stage."

She shudders at the thought. "I don't know why they would think that would happen."

He holds her tight. "Say what you want about big city living, Maddie, but if there's one thing living in a small town has taught me, it's that community cares and you can't find a substitute for that."

He pulls her to him and kisses her again. She never wants their kiss to stop, but it does. He slowly makes a fist and taps the underside of her chin all flirty and soft. "As for World War three, I think you know what they were expecting, and why, Rocky."

She sticks out her tongue at him. "Yo, Adrian. We gonna get hitched, or what?"

He tosses his head back and laughs again before he looks her in the eye, all serious. "As soon as possible, Dill Pickle. I can't wait to be your French Fry."

She giggles. "Okay, then."

He looks a little embarrassed. "Um, Maddie?"

"Yeah."

"There might be an article that's in with your articles that you didn't write."

She has no idea what he's saying. "What are you talking about?"

He rolls his eyes. "Your meet-cute articles. I may have written one in case you never talked to me again." His eyes sparkle and shine. "I still had things to say to you and I didn't know if you would listen, so I put them in your paper."

Her jaw drops. "I may have written one for you, too."

He breaks out in an even bigger grin. "Really? You wrote me an article in the paper?"

She gives him a little love shove. "Well, you wrote me one."

He shakes his head back and forth. "Man, our kids will have one heck of a story about their parents someday."

She smiles at the thought. "That they will, French Fry. That they will." She squeezes his hand. "Now, what's say we get started on planting cucumbers and potatoes in that hate field so we can make more dill pickles and French fries?"

He holds up his hand for a high five. "I say that's a grand idea, Maddie Dill." He winks at her. "If we can't make it as a traveling journalist and welder, we'll always have our dill pickle and French fry business to fall back on."

She slaps his raised hand. "We could have a food truck and sell 'em on the weekends. We could go state-wide."

He pulls her in for another kiss. "I like your big-city thinking, Maddie Dill. Why not share a little bit of our small town with the rest of the world?" His eyes light up as he looks at her with love in his eyes. "We'll call it Pickles-n-Fries."

Her brown eyes soften as she looks up at him. "And fireflies," she adds.

———

Mason and Maddie have been on the road with their food truck for about a week. She can't believe how Mason's friends, who just became new parents, lent them their food truck for the summer. Or that they didn't mind his putting a whole new paint job on it. On his dime of course, but still.

Running a food truck has been a learning experience. She is so thankful to have him by her side. They only make two things but it's hard work and it's exhausting. Being with Mason lightens the load. Maddie knows she couldn't have found a better life partner. When she gets too fired up, he calms her down. If they have an irate customer, she's the muscle.

She takes the trash to the dumpster with a smile as she turns back to look at the cheesy drawing on the side of their midnight blue painted food truck. A giant dill pickle and a giant French fry hold an open jar of fireflies between them as they gaze up at a full moon. Maddie gets all mushy inside all over again when she thinks of how Mason took her dream and turned it into a reality. Maddie knows Mason French will always be the perfect guy for her. He understands her for the small-town girl she is, but he loves her for the big-city girl she longs to be.

They'll have the food truck until November. She figures

that's enough time to see plenty of city life as well as gather souvenirs for their upcoming wedding in the spring. They haven't picked a site or a venue, but Maddie's not worried. She's found the right groom, and that's enough for her.

MYSTERY COUPLE

I ONLY WANT
TO BE YOUR FRENCH FRY

You were my best friend in the whole world. We grew up as close as next-door neighbors can even though an age-old family feud tried to keep us apart. We even had a parcel of land between us called the hate field complete with a surrounding hate fence, but you never saw it that way. That fence was a test of agility and speed to you, my champion. You didn't see it as something that separated us. To you it was just another challenge, something to cross and defeat, which you did in your usual winning way.

You were by my side for every playground fight, every awkward junior high moment, and most every high school dance.

I can't tell you the exact moment you walked away with my heart, only that you've always had it and I don't want it back. I just want you, Dill Pickle. I've been a lone French Fry for too long. Something's missing and I know what it is. I need you beside me. I miss my best friend. You're the only girl who can turn me hot as oil in a fryin' pan in less than two seconds. I'm not the same without you.

Marry me, Maddie Dill, and you'll never have to answer, "Do you want fries with that?" because you'll always have me, your one-and-only French Fry.

- Mason French
The Daily Chase

MYSTERY COUPLE

I'VE BEEN ONE
SOUR DILL PICKLE

My momma always told me I was hard to love. I'm not sure she meant it as a compliment, but I took it as one. I am who I am and I'm afraid I won't change, but there are some good things about dill pickles. Their taste never changes. They're impossible to disguise and there's nothing you can do to change who they are. They stay the same no matter the situation or whose hands they are in.

They might be unattractive with lots of bumps, but they're juicy on the inside. Take one bite and you're addicted. A dill pickle's as good at the beginning as it is at the end. The only thing that makes it better is the occasional flower, a little spice, and a lot of heat. Throw those in with a lot of lovin' and you got yourself the perfect Dill Pickle, and that's what I want to be for you, French Fry. Lots of things go with dill pickles, but French fries go the best. I've found my forever better half in you, and I'm done running.

I love you, Mason French, and I'm not afraid to say it.

- Maddie Dill
The Daily Chase

About the Author

I live in the beautiful Flint Hills of Kansas. I'm blessed to do two things I love- nursing and writing. I have wonderful family support including my husband, our son, daughter-in-law, and two daughters, as well as many friends who willingly give their input whenever it is requested. I'm thankful for the characters and stories as they come along, as well as the companies who publish them and readers who read them.

facebook.com/RachelAnneJonesAuthor

twitter.com/Jones1974Ra

instagram.com/diari197

tiktok.com/@idreamofdandelions

Also by Rachel Anne Jones

With Satin Romance

A Joy-Filled Christmas

Pickles-N-Fries and Fireflies

———

With Fire & Ice YA Books

Novels

Marmalade Uncapped

Essence of Emma

Lovestruck: Kisses, Lies & Oatmeal Cream Pies

All Or Nothing Series

Chasing Denver

Rough Terrain

A Firm Plateau

Radioactive Series

Love and Armageddon

House of Cinders

M.I.A.

www.ingramcontent.com/pod-product-compliance
Lightning Source LLC
Chambersburg PA
CBHW032045240626
47154CB00003B/1086